Lucy's Men

By Lynn Ray Lewis

ISBN-10# 1-945012-71-4
ISBN-13# 978-1-945012-71-6

Artwork by Alexis Belle

Published by Vinvatar Publishing
Website: Vinvatar.com

Table of Contents

Prologue

Scott could probably recite the lecture that his friend Randal Murphy was giving them. The words would be different, but the subject and his solution never changed. Maybe the man thought that if he repeated his thoughts and wishes often enough, the rest of them would give in and agree to hire a surrogate to give each man a child. He could hardly wait to excuse himself from the room. He was in no hurry to procreate, unlike his friends. They had familial obligations to create a new generation of Murphy's and Cummings. He understood their dilemma, but he couldn't identify with them in his life. Thankfully the lecture was winding down.

"Let's face it, women fight. They get all pissy at each other and will peck the eyes out of their best friend if one is prettier than the other, or heavier, or what the fuck ever. They have to have a common enemy in order to get along, and it's usually some sad male who has no idea what kind of trouble he's in. When the man in question and his woman kiss and make-up, the fight is on because one woman is happy and the other is alone; they no longer have a topic of derision that unites them. I've seen it time and again, and I want nothing to do with it. The women no longer have a common enemy; they are the enemies. It sucks, and maybe it isn't always what happens, but I won't take the chance. I want to be happy," Randal Murphy said his piece and lifted his beer to his lips to wet his dry mouth. They'd been hashing and re-hashing this subject for months.

The three men were best friends, business partners, and lovers. Their relationship was unique due to the fact that all three men were bi-sexual. They loved each other, and they enjoyed sex with a woman as equally as they loved to indulge in each other's bodies. They had a pact that no other men would be brought into their circle, and the rules had been adhered to since high school. It might seem strange to others, but others didn't count as far as they were concerned.

The decision to hire a surrogate to give them children was a big stumbling block. Bolt was the last male in his family line, and his parents refused to stop throwing eligible females his way. He was getting tired of having to give the 'it's not you, it's me' speech to every woman his parents lured in to meet their unmarried son. They knew he was bi, and they were doing everything they could think of to get him with a woman so that they could get some grandchildren, including dangling the family fortune in front of them.

He'd finally promised his father that he would take his obligation of fathering the next generation of Cummings children more seriously, and make it a priority. Someone had to carry on the family name and inherit the family fortunes if, and or when, he died.

Looking at the grim-faced Randal, Scott would bet his next paycheck that he had been reamed by his family too. Misery loved company, and Randal was in a similar position to Bolt. Only it was his grandparents that were applying pressure instead of his absent parents.

His father had knocked up the first eligible female that had laid down and lifted her skirt for the playboy. It had occurred two hours after his parents had threatened to cut him out of the will unless he stopped his philandering and gave them a grandchild. Kenneth Murphy hadn't stopped at just one woman that month, the ass had enjoyed deflowering four virgins, that were barely of legal age, in the short span of four weeks.

He'd hedged his bets, and the first girl that admitted she was pregnant got the gold ring. The other three women got the Murphy last name for their children and several thousand dollars per year in maintenance money. They were never excluded from family get togethers and were well loved by their doting grandparents and siblings. As luck would have it. Randal was the only male from the four encounters, and while the girls were adored, the lone male was the future hope for the family name and line.

Scott felt sorry for his friends. He came from the blue-collar working class and was damn glad that his family never pressured him for anything. Well, anything but money. They were too busy doing their damnedest to keep their heads above water economically to worry about who was having babies or who decided to remain childless.

His siblings had several children to fill his mother's grandchild needs. The Henderson name would live long and continue for generations, and Scott would never have to feel compelled to participate in seeding the new generation unless he wanted to.

He wanted a kid, maybe two, but he would rather wait until he found someone that he knew would make a great mom. He made good money from the bars and his investments, so any woman that he picked to carry his children would not be forced to choose between working or taking care of her own kids. His mother had done her best to be all things for her family, and she was still taking care of everyone at home. She didn't work in the factory anymore, but she still washed laundry for his unmarried brothers that lived at home.

He had two brothers in the Marines, and they planned to be lifers in the Corp. One of his sisters was married to a bum, who continuously asked for money, but refused to work toward helping his own situation. His baby sister was graduating from a community college in another month and wanted to go to a four-year university to finish her degree in criminal justice. He had promised her that he would pay her tuition as long as she got decent grades and kept her shit together instead of partying every weekend. It was a good thing that he had faith in the kid and began putting money aside for the tuition because he was going to be writing a hefty check very soon. Melly had surpassed his hopes for her, and he would help her fulfill her dream.

He stood up and grabbed his keys. "I need to get to the club, Aaron is sick tonight, so I'll have to fill in for his routine." He eyed his friends and grinned. "Unless one of you want to volunteer?"

The shaking heads confirmed what he already knew. He didn't mind stripping for the ladies, but the other two hated it. They had each strutted their stuff on stage over the years while they were building their businesses, but once they were established, neither of them volunteered to dance for dollars unless no one else was available. "We still need a bartender for the late shift, so it's up to you to decide who comes in. I'll be too busy." He grinned, shook his head, and waved goodbye on his way out.

Chapter 1

Lucy Posey hung out in the ladies room for as long as she could get away with it. She was with some other women from the shop to celebrate her birthday, as was tradition, but no matter how many times she'd been here, she still felt out of place and uncomfortable. Her friend grabbed her arm, as she was dodging through tables and screaming women, and pulled her over to a ringside table.

"We're here to have fun and enjoy the show, so sit back and admire the best male flesh this planet has to offer." Nicky bought her a mixed drink that tasted like fruit punch and made her want to dance around the room without a partner. The second drink gave her the confidence to whoop and yell along with the other women, as each well-developed male body was revealed.

Not that it would be a big deal if she danced; there were several women already dancing around doing their own thing. Some women had been pulled down from the tables they had climbed on to dance.

The neon lighting advertised this weekend as Hunter's Widow Week. While their men were hunting animals in the woods, the wives were able to view, and even touch, the smooth, muscled bodies of a different kind of animal.

The male strippers kept the women in panting, giggling happiness..

The man on stage was without a doubt the sexiest guy that she had ever seen. Defined muscles undulated under his smooth skin, and she gasped as their eyes met. She was sure that she hadn't seen him here before. He wasn't a man that any woman would be able to forget. He suddenly fell to his hands and knees and began slowly crawling toward her, never taking his eyes from hers, and she felt trapped.

The crowd of women screamed even louder as the man wearing a G-string and nothing but skin, appeared to be in stalking mode. His head was not bowed. Instead his face stared forward, and his golden eyes fascinated his prey. Lucy could barely breathe, let alone stand up and flee. This man, with his wide shoulders and shaggy brown hair, could cause her to have a heart attack if he came any closer, and he kept coming.

Nicky jumped down from her perch on her chair and squeezed Lucy's shoulder, laughing as she said, "I bring you here for your birthday, I buy you a drink, and you catch the eye of the sexiest beast in the place. Not fair girlie, not fair at all."

Lucy couldn't force her eyes to look away from the man that was now less than eight feet away from where she sat, all she could do was shake her head. Her throat was dry, and she knew that the thin t-shirt she wore was showing

her hardened nipples, but the gush of wetness that she felt sliding from her pussy was no joking matter. His nostrils flared as if he could smell the desire that he'd inspired, and the knowing smile, revealing white teeth, and his narrowed eyes, proved that he had indeed caught her scent.

He was two feet from her folded arms resting on the table, and she whimpered. Nicky and Laurie screamed encouragement to her as he held out his hand to Lucy. "Come with me, be mine."

How she found the guts to raise her hand and place it in his was anyone's guess. All she knew was that she wanted this man, even knowing that he probably did this for a living with countless women. There was something about him that called to her from deep inside. He might not be Mr. Right, but he was Mr. Right Now, and in the mood she was in, he could be Mr. Fuck-Me-Until-We-Can't-Walk.

His hands pulled her from her seat, dragged her over the table, and up onto the stage. He stopped pulling her arms once her head was even with his own. Their kiss was sloppy, crazy, and carnal. His tongue mapped her mouth and licked down her jaw to the sensitive spot under her ear lobe. He was breathing hard, and she licked at his skin, tasting the flavored oil coating his sun-kissed hide.

His shaggy hair hid their faces from the audience, and she barely heard him telling her to "hang on." She continued to lick and kiss his delicious skin. When she took his nipple between her teeth and began to nibble, his hands clasped thick handfuls of her blonde hair. "Stop that. My cock is as hard as a damned rock for you, and if you keep it up, we'll be fucking right here for all of these camera phones to see. As it is, I have no idea how long it will take to calm down enough to not to give the ladies a real show." His forehead leaned down to rest on hers. "G-strings aren't built to contain a cock like mine when it's hard. Getting off of the stage will be next to impossible without something to cover me up."

His teeth showed as laughter rumbled out of his throat. The man was laughing at his predicament, and she grinned back at him. She didn't see the problem from her position, but her sex fogged brain finally registered that it could be a potentially embarrassing situation.

The lights blinked twice, and the emergency lighting kicked on within seconds. Scott looked towards the bar and saw Randal wave him off of the darkened stage. He wasted no time pulling his body up and got ready to rush away from his audience. He was not about to leave the woman that made his dick hard with one glance. She stumbled a little as he hauled her up and towed her from the sight of prying eyes.

They made their way down the back steps off of the stage and went directly down the narrow hallway until they came to a door that said Office. He pushed his lush female captive ahead of him into the room.

Lucy found herself sinking into the cool material covering a couch in the dimly lit room. She caught a glimpse of his cock and knew that she needed to slow him down a bit. She was not a virgin, but her former boyfriend definitely lacked in the quick comparison that she couldn't help but make. This man was built like a fantasy.

"*Oh hell, why are you chickening out you've always dreamed of being with a well-endowed man. Just shut the fuck up and enjoy the experience. It's not like men like this are breaking down your door every day.*" The little pep talk with herself helped to put her nagging worry aside. She never stepped out of the box; maybe it was time she tried it. She licked her lips and raised her arms to encircle his wide shoulders.

Her shirt was being pulled over her head at the same time, and it made her giggle as she attempted to pull her arms loose. "This should be as easy as the books say it is." He didn't answer her observation. His lips were traveling down her chest and latching onto her nipple. The tug on her flesh signaled pleasure to her lower body, and another gush of wetness slipped from her pussy.

Once her shirt was tossed aside, and her bra had been dealt with amidst more embarrassed giggles and gasps, his hands went to the snap of her shorts.

Scott raised his head and waited for her to focus on his face before talking to her. He knew that she wasn't drunk, so that didn't concern him. His worries leaned more to the practical side.

"Hey, I need to know a couple of things before this goes further." He stole a quick kiss from her moist lips that she kept licking. "I have a rule I never break, so you need to tell me if you have a husband or are in a serious relationship that you will be going back to when you leave here. I don't see a ring, but that doesn't mean much nowadays to some people."

She let his words sink in and shook her head no. "He wanted his skinny neighbor more than he wanted me." She tried to sit up, but his thick shoulders held her in place, lying on the cushion as his hand pulled at the material of her shorts. "By the way, my name is Lucy."

She didn't know what was so different about this man, but she wanted him deep inside of her body, and she wanted him to know who he was fucking for the night. Maybe he would remember her the next time he picked a woman from his audience to screw. The thought of him licking and sucking another woman's skin like he was doing to hers flat pissed her off. Why he chose her was still a puzzle, but as far as she was concerned, tonight they were committed to having mind-blowing sex, and she would live with the consequences later.

She was completely bare within seconds, and she loved seeing the way her fantasy man looked at her. His nostrils flared, and his eyes never strayed from her. His hands mapped her from neck to knee, and her heart thumped so hard in her chest that she could swear he must be able to hear its beat.

"You are the sexiest woman I've ever seen in here. I don't know why you decided to walk into the bar, and I don't care what it takes out of me to make you want to come back for more. You need to tell me what you want, or if I do something you don't like, tell me." He cupped her jaw and made sure that her eyes were focused enough to assure him that she understood what he said to her. "Nod your head if you remember what I just said. Do you want this?"

She nodded and turned her head enough to bite the side of his thumb that was closest to her lips. She whispered the words he wanted to hear, "No regrets."

As far as he was concerned, it was enough. He leaned down over her and took her breasts in both hands. There was more than a mere handful, and he loved pulling the thick nipples into hard pebbles for his lips to suck. Soon, his lips traveled down her stomach, and over her padded hip bones. Her mound wasn't bare, but the hair was trimmed; that didn't stop him from finding the slit of her pussy and splitting it with his thumbs.

Her clit was exposed, and from the way the tiny muscle peeked from its hooded cave, he knew that she wanted him as much as he needed her. His tongue swatted the tiny muscle, and she raised her hips screaming low in her throat. The sound egged him on. His lips closed onto her clit, and he sucked hard, before lashing at the very tip with his tongue.

Lucy couldn't have stopped if she wanted to. Feeling his mouth on her was an education, and a pleasure, that she wouldn't want to miss. Not only was his mouth torturing her clit in the most enjoyable way, but he'd also stuck two fingers inside of her slick pussy. She could feel herself clasping those digits with every movement of his lips. Her orgasm peaked, stringing her out stiff, and she raised her hips and most of her body to shove into his caress as she yelled out her pleasure.

She was still gasping for breath as his thickness began to enter her. His advance and retreat rhythm allowed her body to stretch in small increments, and as she looked down at the spot where his cock was joining her needy pussy, she pulled herself up by clasping his thick neck. Her teeth grazed his shoulder, and she wanted to bite down but knew she would draw blood if she did. Instead, she sucked at his collar bone. She had no control over her fingers digging into his back, or the way she tried to rise and meet his invasion into the welcoming wet heat of her body. The noises

that came from her throat were more animal than feminine, but she needed this.

Hands pulled her bloody fingernails from the warmth of his back and urged her to lay back onto the cushions. The hands soothing her face and brushing her hair out of her eyes were not the ones that currently held her hips up while her pussy clasped around the wide cock that slid deep inside.

She didn't understand what was happening at first, but once she understood that there were more than just the two of them in the room, her eyes widened, and she opened her mouth to tell the intruder to get the hell out of there. The words never left her mouth. The man that was smiling at her was as handsome as her stripper, and he leaned down to place a tender kiss on the side of her lips.

"I won't hurt you, but you were ripping the hide off of Scott when I came in, and we can't have our main attraction all clawed up." He kept peppering her face with kisses; light, barely felt kisses, but they were effective in calming her panic.

"I wish I had seen you first, but if you say so, I believe that this will be a night that you will remember for quite some time." He licked her lip and returned to give her a deeper kiss. "What do you say? Will you allow us to give you the best night of your life?"

He couldn't have timed his request better. Scott must have hit her happy place deep inside of her pussy. Her eyes widened, and she reached for his hand to bring it to her breast. Randal smiled and gave the beautiful flesh a squeeze and a quick pinch on the nipple. She gasped, and her back bowed even more, as she groaned.

He quickly pulled the shirt from his back and unfastened his trousers, allowing them to hit the floor. Her curious little fingers were tangled in his chest hair before he could pull them away, and he lost several strands as he pried her fingers loose.

"Hey, kitten, you are evil with those damn claws. You need something to keep them busy, and from the way you're licking your lips, I think I've got just what you need here." He smiled as he pinched both of her hard nipples. "Look at me, I want to make sure you understand and want this as much as I do." Her eyes found his, even as her lids slid to half-mast and her mouth opened on a wail of pleasure.

He nodded and pulled the erect nipples between his fingers one more time. "Okay, kitten, you can have my cock to suck on if you want, but if you bite, I will not be happy, and I will bust that beautiful ass of yours." He leaned down to kiss her quickly, as he felt the pre-cum slide through the slit in the head of his cock when she licked her lips and zeroed her sights in on his hard length.

He went to his knees next to her head and jumped as her warm mouth latched onto the dark pink head of his dick. He groaned and ran his hand over her head.

"It's so good; you suck my cock like you've been starved. Slow down, kitten; I'm not going anywhere." He looked toward Scott and enjoyed the sight of the man's thick cock splitting the lips of her damp pussy.

Scott grinned at Randal and winked as he nodded towards their evenings' entertainment. "She's tight, and she's fuckin' beautiful. Her pussy is sucking my cock every time I pull back. It's incredible." He kissed the inside of the knee that was lying over his shoulder. "I can't hold back much longer, so be prepared for her to move, cause I'm going deep, and she's primed to take me there."

Randal watched as Scott slowly sped up his thrusts, going deeper with each down stroke. The grunts and noises that their kitten was making was giving him reason to worry about spilling his cum before either of them came. That was unacceptable. He knew that as soon as Scott bottomed out, she would either scream in discomfort or ecstasy.

He watched as she lifted her hips even higher for the cock that was pleasuring her wet cunt. Her scream came, but it was due to the orgasm that strung her body stiff in mid-air while Scott shoved as deep as his prick would go, and stayed in position while she jerked and cried out around the cock in her mouth.

Randal pulled his cock from her mouth. She began grinding her teeth, moaning from her throat, and he was glad that she hadn't latched down on his tender flesh. She was still gasping for breath when he felt her hand clasp his wet cock and pet it for a moment before she licked her lips and sucked the head back into the warmth of her mouth. The noises and tight clamp of her lips made the cum begin to flow from his cock and into the back of her throat. It was his turn to jerk and gasp, but she egged him on with her fingers teasing and pinching the sac of his balls.

Scott had given in to the pleasure of her pussy clamping down rhythmically as soon as the initial orgasm hit her. He stayed buried deep inside until his cock began to retreat from its warm, tight spot. Seeing Randal come into the office while he was engaged with, *"Wait; her name. She said her name was what? Lacey? No, Lucy,"* yes, Lucy had been a gift tonight, and she had taken him without any pretense.

It had been a wildly erotic sight when Randal offered up his hard cock for her to enjoy. The way that her pussy was still clasping his meat told him that she liked and gained pleasure from sucking Randal into a limp mess. Some women enjoyed bringing a man to his knees, and it seemed that Lucy was one of them.

Scott pulled away from her quivering body and stood to remove the condom before the damn thing fell off on its own. He hated wearing them, but he would hate contacting some nasty disease even worse. Not to mention, pregnancy. This one had broken loose at the base. At first, it alarmed him. The ring was still around the thickest part of the root of his cock, and along the side about an inch up it had split. His cum was safe in the tip; he wondered if the way Lucy had jerked around at the height of her orgasm had twisted the normally skin-tight latex into tearing.

All he could do was hope that it was not her fertile time of the month and that the pouch of semen stayed intact. It had been a damn miracle that he'd remembered to grab a condom in the first place. He'd rolled it over his cock even as his dick was leaking pre-cum. "*Fuck; just fuck.*" It was stupid of him to have let his need for her drive common sense from his brain.

Lucy laid on the couch spread-eagle and limp. She allowed herself a few moments of euphoric afterglow, before remembering that she didn't even know the stripper's name or the second man's name.

"*You know that you fucked up tonight, right?*" Asking herself for confirmation of her stupidity helped to sober her from the sexual haze that had been so enjoyable. It was time to beat a hasty retreat and go home to drown in remorse. She had a feeling that her biggest regret about this evening was going to be that she would never get to repeat her mistake with taking on these two strange men.

She sat up and groaned. The stripper held her shirt out towards her, and she almost snatched it from his hand. While she pulled the shirt over her head, she heard the door open and close, and she hoped that the men had left, but once her head popped through the neckline, she saw that only half of her wish had come true. One man remained, and he was frowning at her.

She avoided his gaze by searching the floor for her denim shorts and shoes. Her keys and cash were in the pocket of the shorts because she hated carrying a purse into a bar. Not that she had much money to worry about getting stolen, but what she did have she'd earned, and did her best to use it wisely. Even to celebrate her birthday with the women that worked on the assembly line that she was the lead on, she'd budgeted for. Nicky had insisted on this outing, and Lucy couldn't come up with a reason good enough to avoid it. It was her birthday, and she hadn't been out in almost a year.

She shook her head. *You couldn't just have a few drinks, ogle a few sexy men, and go home, could you? Nope, you had to go all out for this one.* Turning twenty-eight wasn't the end of the world. As far as memorable milestones in life, this one would definitely make her top ten.

She looked up when the second guy cleared his throat. He was nodding towards the table on the furthest end of the room. Her shorts were hanging from the lampshade. She hated to walk over to the lamp, but the smiling man standing in front of the large wooden desk didn't appear to be in a hurry to retrieve them for her. She yanked the t-shirt down as far as possible and scurried over to the table lamp. Her thong wasn't with the denim, but right now, she wasn't going to spend time looking for it. She felt the lumps in her pockets that confirmed that her keys and small, folding, wallet were still there. Now all she needed was the canvas slides for her feet, and she could walk out the door.

She wanted to act casual about stumbling into her shorts, but there was nothing graceful about the way she overbalanced and landed sideways on the over- stuffed couch. The wish that she could slink out the door and disappear didn't happen. She rested her head on her arm for a minute. For some reason, all she wanted to do was laugh. A small giggle escaped, and that little sound let the floodgates open wide. She laughed and cried at the same time. Whatever happened the rest of the night would be blamed on Karma.

This not so graceful repair to her clothes had to be Karma's doing. "I bet it's because I laughed at Murray for losing his false teeth in the grinder. It's payback; it doesn't matter that today is my birthday. Nope, fate has a way of showing up at the least convenient times. Maybe I should just sit here bare-assed and wait for my next bad decision."

Lucy didn't realize that she'd spoken out loud until she heard the quiet masculine laughter. "Okay, Karma, I'm humbled. I am a pitiful human being, and you have made your point." She raised her hands and let them drop to the cushion. "Can you help me find my shoes so I can leave with a little dignity?" She hastily added a, "Please," before trying to pull her shorts up and over her wide hips without standing for the stranger's entertainment.

She wiggled until the denim covered her ass, and decided that the only way to fasten the darn things would be to roll over, or stand up. Peeking over the back of the sofa was a mistake. Tall, dark, and handsome was standing right there. Still naked.

He had probably been watching her wiggle and struggle to get dressed too. Dangling from his fingers were her shoes. At least, he was smiling. She took a deep breath and decided that she couldn't embarrass herself much more, so she stood up and turned to face him.

She snapped her shorts and zipped her finger in the teeth of the short closure; then she gave up. Reaching out for her shoes, she had to lean over the couch to take them from the man with the delicious cock. She could still taste him, and she was fighting her nature with every bit of dignity that she could muster.

All she wanted to do was move in close to his bare chest, and cuddle. That was her problem, she was a touchy-feely type, and men hated clingy women. Why she wanted to cuddle up to a stranger was just one more reason for her to get the hell out of here quick. Looking into his teasing eyes, and glancing at that wide expanse of tanned, thickly padded muscle, made her mouth go dry.

She snatched the shoes and muttered, "Thank you," as she hobbled around, getting her shoes on the right feet without killing herself. Heading for the door proved to be another challenge. There were three doors in the room, and she had no idea which one they'd come into the room from.

"I realize that you might be feeling a little awkward, but do you think that you might tell me what your name is? I'm not in the habit of having sex with women that I haven't met before, or even just letting her suck my cock."

She knew that her face was beet red, and she choked out her name as she headed for a door with a light switch next to the door jamb. "I'm Lucy, nice meeting you." Thankfully the door opened into a noisy hallway, and she almost ran through the opening. She rushed past the bathrooms and ran into Nicky.

She grinned and took the teasing about disappearing with the handsome stripper. "He's great, a really nice guy. I need to get going home now; I have some errands that need to get done in the morning, so I'll see you on Monday."

Babbling to the beautiful brunette was a wasted effort. Nicky was eyeing a beefy red-haired stripper, and she waved Lucy off as she moved towards the stage.

That was easier than I thought it would be. She wove her way to the front doors. Finally seated inside of her car with the doors locked, she started lecturing herself and didn't stop until she parked in the driveway. She'd learned a long time ago not to talk to herself while people were around; they just didn't understand. Some of them acted like she wasn't too bright mentally when they saw or heard her conversations. The way that she had been raised had everything to do with her bad habit of speaking what was on her mind, no matter who was around.

Her grandparents had raised her, and since both of the elders were deaf as doorposts, refusing to spend the money on hearing aids, she'd lived in silence at home. On the rare occasions that her grandparents felt the need to communicate, they yelled at one another and at Lucy too. To this day, she hated it when people raised their voices in her direction.

They also didn't believe in modern conveniences such as a television. She felt fortunate that her grandmother liked music. The fact that the music had to be turned up so loudly that the cheap speakers vibrated, often distorting the sound of the music, gave her an appreciation for the radio in her car. It wasn't fancy, but the sound was exceptional compared to what she'd been forced to listen to at home.

She knew just about every country and western song that had been played on that old radio. That knowledge had often allowed her to win concert tickets from the local radio stations. Many times she had invited another shy girl to go with her to enjoy the concert. Other times, she gave the tickets to classmates, when she wasn't particularly interested in seeing the show. Most of the time she just answered the trivia questions to make herself feel smart.

School had been her salvation and showed her a truth about herself. She hated the classes but loved the interaction with others. Music class was a mixed blessing. She had a good singing voice, but not being able to read the words, well, that created problems for her. The teacher thought that she was being defiant, and like most of the other teachers sent her to the office.

Kids are cruel, but not as cruel as teachers that are burnt out from too many students with learning disabilities, or students that feel entitled to good grades whether deserved or not. It had been her English teacher that discovered that Lucy was dyslexic, and she had done her best to help Lucy overcome the hell of not understanding what she tried so desperately to grasp.

She had barely graduated from high school and had grabbed the first manufacturing job that didn't require more reading than she could cope with. Numbers had always been easy for her to understand, but give her a five letter word and she got frustrated. She had been with the same company for almost ten years now, and she was proud of the way she'd advanced through the ranks.

She never told anyone that the local community college had given classes at night on how to help children with reading disabilities, and by the third class, the professor had figured out what Lucy was doing there.

Five years later, Kendra had become her trusted friend. They didn't pal around because the teacher's husband was an ass. She never stopped at Kendra's house; they usually met at the college or at the coffee shop after Kendra finished teaching her last class of the night. She didn't serve as a teacher to Lucy nowadays. In fact, after next month, she would see Kendra even less since the older woman was pregnant with her third child. It was one more change that this year had brought.

Earlier this year, her boyfriend of six years had decided that his neighbor, a woman with a rich daddy and string bikini, was a better prospect than Lucy's dirt poor grandparents, and her curvy figure. It was sad when she realized that the only thing she missed about Tony was having someone around to talk to her.

She noticed that it was almost one in the morning. "Way past bedtime, girlie. You are breaking all kinds of rules tonight, aren't you?"

She laughed at her own dumb ass. Staying up late was the least of her transgressions for the evening. She headed for the shower; if she didn't wash the scent of the men from her body, she would never get any sleep tonight.

Chapter 2

Scott almost ran back to the office as soon as he'd broken up the fight between four drunken women in the bar. The transition from removing a broken condom to hearing the screams and looking up to see the red light that signaled trouble to the occupants of the office on any given night, had pushed his good mood away faster than he'd run into the fray. It had taken ten minutes to calm the ladies, and giving them access to Bill and Oliver, had been a last ditch solution before calling the cops. Luckily, the two men were up for the challenge, and everyone was grinning before Scott turned around to go back to the office.

He shook his head at his choice of grabbing Randall's jeans on his way out of the door to cover his naked ass. Randall was two inches taller than he was, and wider in every way; the swish, swish sound as he walked made him smile. As he made his way through the crowd, he felt several feminine hands patting his ass and lower back. The ladies expressing concern about the claw marks on his shoulders were given smiles and winks. The furrows burned, but he liked it. He had one hand holding the pants up enough to keep from letting them drop to the floor while his other hand helped move aside women that were in his path.

His Lucy was passionate, and she tasted great. It had been quite a while since he'd tasted and fucked a woman half as desirable as the pretty blonde. The instant attraction had taken him off guard for sure. He hoped that Randal had been keeping her warmed up for round two, and felt his cock stir in anticipation. He wanted her almost as desperately now as he had the first round.

Randal was sitting behind the desk when Scott opened the door and rushed inside. He came to a halt with his hands on the jeans button. Looking around, it was obvious that Lucy wasn't in the room, and the open bathroom door proved that she hadn't hidden inside that small space. He didn't have to ask; Randal was already telling him how the girl had slipped away so easily.

"If you hadn't swiped my jeans, I would have followed her, and tried to get her number or something. You know damned well that I can't even fit one of my legs in your fucking pants."

Randal had a point. It didn't ease Scott's disappointment, but his explanation was legitimate. Randal was huge. His body was a disciplined mass of muscle that had been toned to perfection. His thighs were thick, and that ass was a work of art. His calves were bigger than Scott's biceps, and he was correct, there was no way that he would fit in Scott's clothes.

"Luckily enough, we have the video feed from the bar tonight, and I have been going through the receipts on the nights take to see if our kitten used a credit card. We can track her down that way." He gave Scott a lopsided grin, "Did you happen to notice that she talks to herself a lot?"

At four in the morning, the men admitted defeat. There was no evidence that a woman named Lucy had used a charge card. The video feed from the bar and stage showed two women interacting with the woman that was eluding the men's efforts to gather information about her. The women paid their waiter in cash, so that avenue of discovery was out.

Scott was tired, and he was staring at Lucy's face on the computer screen. "I want her; whatever it takes, I want this one." He looked at Randal and nodded. "I know it's fucked up, and crazy as hell, but the minute I laid eyes on her, my heart dropped right there in front of her." He blew out a breath and stretched his neck before re-focusing his gaze on the monitor.

Randal typed a few words on the keyboard and hit the print feature. The machine spit out an eight by ten of Lucy's face and the next page held pictures of the two women that they'd identified as her companions.

"Tomorrow we can ask the staff and the guys if anyone knows the women, or if they are frequent customers. If they've been here before, the guys will know them. Bill likes the brunette's body type, and you know that Wilson always presses his luck with the freckled ones." The next picture of Lucy, he gave to Scott.

"Here you go; you can stare at this on the ride home. We'll leave the bike in the shed, and you can ride with me." He walked forward wearing nothing but a soft t-shirt and a smile. "Now, how about you hand me my pants, or we can make the bed up here and spend the night, or at least, what's left of it, right here." His jeans sailed over Scott's shoulder, and he laughed, "Chicken."

They checked to make sure that no one lingered under a table or was passed out in the bathroom, before locking up and setting the alarm. It had started to rain, and both men raised their faces to allow the rain to wash away the fatigue they felt.

It was a good thing that Randal drove a rugged SUV that didn't require pampering. The men were soaked by the time they ran across the parking lot and got the doors unlocked. Lightning and thunder were increasing in intensity, and the wind had begun howling before they drove into the garage at home.

Bolt was watching the news station when they squished their way into the house. It was not unusual to find him like that. The shattered torment displayed on his face told his friends that something bad had happened. They looked towards the television for answers and saw what had gotten his attention.

There were images of the remains of a downed airplane. Unusual yes, but the house that the plane had landed on explained everything. There was no mistaking the location as anything but Bolt's childhood home. Instead of the eighteen ninety Queen Ann Victorian, monster-sized home, there were flames shooting from a gaping hole in the center of the dwelling. Fire trucks surrounded the scene, but there appeared to be nothing left to save. The front porch that the family had gathered on during warm summer evenings was the only thing left of the house. Scott grabbed the remote and silenced the ongoing commentary about the death toll.

The running message along the bottom of the screen blamed sheer winds, and lightning from the severe storm, for downing the plane. Over one hundred people were believed to have died in the crash, including the home's occupants. Randal picked up Bolt's phone when it rang, and fielded the questions from the caller. His "no comment" answer became repetitive as the calls continued to ring in.

Fatigue completely forgotten, the three men drove over to the scene of the accident but had to walk three blocks in order to speak to the fire chief and to the police officer in charge. There were cars and emergency vehicles all over the road, blocking any incoming traffic, but the EMT's had very few people needing their

services. A few burns and scrapes from the firefighters was about the worst injuries at the scene. Anyone involved in the wreck had been incinerated, or impossible to find and rescue alive.

The water hoses continued to soak the pile of rubble, but most of the emergency responders were packing up equipment, and some were leaving since they were not needed. The news crew continued to attempt to get anyone within the vicinity to talk to them about the fire and wreck, and when they approached Bolt while he spoke with the fire chief, Scott and Randal blocked their way.

"Look, lady, he doesn't want to talk to you. I know it's your job to get a story, but you should leave him alone tonight."

Scott's advice was ignored. The vulture had gotten sight of prey, and she was not about to allow this chance to show her viewers' the grief on Bolton Cummings face to slip away. She screeched when Randal grabbed the lens off of the camera that her companion was hanging on to. He twisted the lens off without causing damage but refused to give into her demands, or the camera man's plea, to return the expensive piece of equipment.

"You already have your story, leave Mr. Cummings alone tonight. His parents are believed to have been in that house, as you well know, so cut him some slack." He shook his head at the determination on the reporter's face. She wanted something that he was not going to allow her to have. "Leave him alone, lady; we aren't moving from this spot until he does."

Her screaming attracted the attention of the police officer in charge, and he came over to see what her damage was. After listening about the rights of the press, and understanding that the stoic men were waiting for him to decide how to deal with the problem, John Murrow raised his hat back on his forehead and smiled at the enraged reporter.

"Now, Ms. Kelly, you sure are a pretty sight to see this early in the morning, that's a fact. I understand that these yahoos' are giving you grief because you don't care about who got hurt, you just want your story." He shot Randal a nod and smirk, "Now, I'll tell you what I'm gonna' do 'cause there's been enough bad news tonight. I'm gonna' make this ol' boy give back the lens, and then I'll kick them out of the area, so you can get your story, and we can finish up here. Then we can all go home and get dry and warm."

Karen Kelly shot Randal a smug look, not realizing Scott had walked back to Bolton Cummings, and that they had already weaved their way through the vehicles until they were out of sight. She screamed again, and Officer Murrow held out his hand towards Randal.

"Now, Mr., you can't go around interrupting a lady reporter like you did, and you're lucky that I'm not in the mood to arrest you unless she presses charges. Hand me the lens, and get out of here. If I see you here again tonight, I'll lock you up." He nodded and smiled, before turning to the cameraman and handing over the piece of equipment. "Here you go, son, all right and tight," he winked at the nervous man, tipped his hat towards Karen Kelly, and walked over to the squad car.

He wouldn't be able to leave the scene until the fire department was certain that everything was safe to leave without supervision. This was going to be a long and messy investigation for sure. He would have to be present when the Feds showed up to investigate tomorrow too. If he was lucky, Woodrow Nelson would show up to relieve him for a few hours. He rested his head back on the padded seat back and settled in for a long morning.

The Cummings family were important people in this town, and who knew who was on that damn plane when it went down. Karen Kelly didn't know it, but she was fortunate that Bolton's friends had intervened on his behalf. If she'd made it to the Cummings heir, he would have smashed her camera and the man carrying it. Bolton was not known for his patience, in fact, he was well known for taking matters into his own hands. He wouldn't have physically harmed the woman, but the man would destroy her career if she pissed him off enough.

John remembered Bolt and his crew from high school; the memories were good ones for the most part. The three men were thicker than brothers in the flesh, and it was no surprise that the friendships had carried over into adulthood. He would call on Bolt in a day or two and deal with whatever came up in the meantime.

Chapter 3

There were so many people at the memorial service for his parents that Bolt wondered if they came out of respect and concern, or out of curiosity. Not that it mattered, he knew many of the people by sight if not name, and he did his best to stay polite in the face of the intrusive questions.

He looked over at Randal and Scott as they ushered ladies from his mother's garden club to their cars. He was grateful to have the two of them to lean on. No man could have better friends, and without them, he would be a grieving mess for the world to see. There had been nothing left of his parents to bury, but their deaths needed to be acknowledged, so a memorial service was the solution for dealing with the public's demand for closure.

He loved his parents dearly and would never understand how they could be dead without even a goodbye. They'd just returned from a vacation in Iceland. His mother had set a goal of vacationing in a new country every year, and his father indulged the woman he'd married when they were twenty years old. The only blessing that Bolt could see in their deaths is that they went together. Remembering the way that they chased each other around the house when no one but family was around, made him smile. He had no doubt that they were still holding hands and laughing together, wherever they were.

That love was the measure for Bolt. If he could find a woman that could take his breath every time she smiled, or hardened his dick the minute he caught the scent of her hair or skin, he'd snatch her up and marry her in the blink of an eye. Frank Cummings had always explained his fascination with the pretty little redhead by blaming her for being irresistible. Penny Cummings, nee Bolton, always kept her loved ones close and made sure that they knew of her love and affection. Bolt would miss her most of all. He was lucky that he had Randal and Scott to keep him sane.

Randal's suggestion of a surrogate to carry children was beginning to look better now than the night that he'd originally explained his reasons for using a surrogate. His parents wanted grandkids, and he felt like he'd cheated them somehow by not producing a few for them to spoil rotten.

He was still weighing the pros and cons of artificially inseminating a strange female when Scott placed a hot mug of coffee in front of him while he sat in the kitchen after the service. Tonight was not the time to reintroduce the subject, but soon, very soon, he would make a decision and stick to it.

Randal came in and tossed his phone on the table before finding a mug and pouring himself half of a cup of the dark roast. He looked at Scott's hopeful face and shook his

head. They'd been discretely looking for Lucy for eight days, and no one at the bar had ever seen her before. Her friend is named Nicky, but that was all anyone could tell them about either woman. Every avenue to discover her identity and whereabouts had been exhausted. Short of putting her picture on milk jugs or beer bottles, they were at a dead end.

Scott scowled and began pulling at his bottom lip. It was a nervous habit that told his friends that his brilliant brain was working overtime. Scott acted like a carefree party boy most of the time, but those close to him knew that the man had a high IQ. He could process numbers and equations faster than a normal person could type them into a calculator. He'd hated school but had two degrees because he wanted to see if he could complete both within a year of each other. His family depended on him far too much, but he found the guts to say no when they tried to take advantage too blatantly.

He finally grinned; even his eyes were slightly squinted. Randal rolled his own eyes, sure that whatever scheme that Scott had worked out was going to involve going door to door asking if anyone had seen Lucy. He groaned when Scott finally told them what he planned to do. It wasn't far off of Randal's guess.

"I'm taking this picture of her and the one of her buddy, and giving them to a few of the dancers at the bar." He grinned showing teeth and determination. "They can make the rounds of neighborhood bars and a few fast food spots. I just remembered that you said she said it was her birthday. Face it; ours is pricier than most places; women go there to celebrate birthdays and divorces. It makes sense. She still has to go out once in a while, even if it's for a burger and fries. Someone knows her; we just need to find the right person."

It made perfect sense, and Randal wished he had thought of it. Right now he figured that he could be forgiven for not being on top of his game. The hour of sexual enjoyment had turned into a night of tragedy, and every waking minute had been filled with helping Bolt cope with the loss of his parents and the paperwork that still was not completed.

Randal was Bolt's attorney on a personal level, but the elder Cummings' had a law firm that dealt with the business and their own personal legal matters. That firm was not happy to know that Randal Murphy represented Bolt. They needed to make certain that all paperwork and information was accurate and ready for scrutiny. So far he had not found any discrepancies, but the partners seemed to become more nervous as each meeting had progressed.

Their behavior gave Randal reason to bring his auditors with him at the last meeting, and it had not been as friendly as the first meeting. The mess could take months to unravel. He hated to think that attorney's that he'd known and admired for years were shady, but Bolt would be protected; that was the bottom line. If they were stealing from his friend, there wouldn't be a rock big enough for them to hide under. Randal would dismantle their office brick by brick in defense of his loved one.

"Okay, we can round up some of the guys tomorrow. I'm too damn tired tonight." He twisted his neck, feeling the bones and muscles stretch and heard the cracking noise as he tilted his head back. "It's been a hell of a week, and I can't see it letting up anytime soon."

Scott watched Randal, and he stood up to walk around the table to begin working the man's brawny shoulders. "Take off the shirt and I'll work you over."

He helped pull the dress shirt from Randal's arms and sighed. "I'm sorry, I tend to forget that you two need more than four hours of sleep and down time." His fingers dug into the thick slabs of muscle, making Randal groan and close his eyes. The gentle push forward caused him to raise his arms and pillow his head on his folded forearms.

"You and Bolt have been taking care of the business end of Frank and Penny's loss, and I've tried to keep the home fires burning here. I keep remembering those blue eyes and everything about that night with her." He shrugged and worked his strong fingers into

Randal's scalp at the neckline. "I'm obsessed, and I know it."

Bolt listened to the one-sided conversation that Scott was carrying on with the weary Randal. Who was this Lucy, and what night was he talking about? This was the first that he'd heard about her.

"Hold on a minute. Who and what are you talking about? You've been holding out on me?"

Randal groaned when Scott stopped working his magic muscle manipulation and walked into the living room. He picked up a picture from the computer printer tray and brought it into the kitchen, laying it in front of Bolt on the table. He went back to his task for Randal, but his eyes stayed on the picture.

"All we know is that her name is Lucy, she talks to herself a lot according to Randal, and she had me by the balls from the minute I looked into her eyes. I'm obsessed, and Randal isn't far behind. Her birthday was the same day of the plane crash, and she disappeared with no trace an hour and a half after we met." He shook his head and leaned down to place a smacking kiss between Randal's shoulder blades. "She took both of us without playing the blushing virgin. And when I tasted her and was inside of her body, it felt like I belonged there."

Talking about the way he felt when his cock slid into her pussy made his dick stretch. The smooth flesh beneath his lips and the groan of enjoyment coming from Randal egged him on. He let his fingertips tease the masculine nipples that hardened immediately at his touch. He continued to tease with his fingers and lips, until Randal pushed back and stood up, turning around to pull him into his powerful embrace.

He enjoyed the feeling of being held so close to the big man's naked chest. He pulled the cotton t-shirt from his own back and rubbed his chest against Randal's. He looked over Randal's shoulder and smiled at Bolt. "You gonna just stand there?"

Bolt shook his head and grinned. "Let's move this to the other room, or the bedroom. We need space tonight, and my cock is about to blow from watching you seduce Randal. You look so fucking sexy licking on his neck and daring me with your eyes to join in."

He headed for the sectional, shedding his suit as he walked. He needed this with Scott and Randal tonight. The closeness, the care, the love. He needed it all in a physical way right now. This past week had been one slice of hell after another, and without these two, well, he didn't want to think about that. He ran to the bedroom to grab some lube and condoms, before coming back in time to see Scott crawl on top of a now naked Randal. They were going to suck each other's cocks, and Bolt stood still, enjoying the sight. He began stroking his own hardness, shivering as he remembered what their mouths felt like on his cock.

Scott began licking his way around the thick meat in his fist, as he felt Randal take a hold of his dick. The hand holding him was big enough to close around his flesh, and he groaned in response to the pleasure from the pressure of the squeezing fingers.

He sucked the skin at the base of Randal's cock, adding a small nip to the sac holding his sensitive balls. His fingers encircled the wide base as he nibbled his way further up towards the head. He hummed as he worked, and loved hearing Randal moan as he raised his hips for more.

Feeling the warmth of Randal's mouth close over the tip of his cock made him tighten his hold on the cock in his hand, and raise his head to moan loudly from the pleasure of sliding tip to balls deep. Randal had no gag reflex, and Scott cried out as Randal made a swallowing motion. When he felt fingers lubing up his ass crack, Scott begged for more.

"Please. Oh God, yes!" His hips were held in place as Bolt reamed his hole with two fingers, and he felt one of them pinching the small spot between his balls and asshole. "Fuck me, yes. Give me what you've got, I love this."

Feeling the lube slicked, latex encased cock enter his body while his cock was deep inside Randal's throat, almost made him pass out. He saw a rainbow of colors behind his closed eyelids, but even as the dizziness passed his breath continued rushing through his lungs. He licked on the cock in his hands, but if he moved down enough to suck and pleasure it with his mouth, he would lose the position that he was in. He used spit to help run his hands up and down the thick cock that became even harder as he pumped it to orgasm.

Bolt seated his cock as deep as he could get in Scott's tight ass. He rested for a moment before beginning to move his hips progressively faster and running his hands up to Scott's shoulders to hold him steady for the hard driving rhythm that was coming. The finger sliding up and into his own ass took away what little control that he might have claimed at that second. He shoved his cock deep three times and yelled out his pleasure while the semen shot into the latex and his cock jumped with the rhythmic clasp of Scott's ass as he orgasmed.

Randal needed to breathe, but he didn't want to shove Bolt from Scott's body, so he used saliva to wet his finger and enter Bolt's back hole. It had been a couple of weeks since they had engaged each other like this, so he knew it wouldn't take much to send him over the edge. Luckily for his breathing, he was correct. Scott came, and Randal swallowed his offering with no hesitation.

As Scott's dick softened, Randal turned his head to catch his breath, while he shot his own load over the wet tongue licking at the dark pink head of his cock. He left his finger inside of Bolt as he felt the telltale throbbing and clasping, signaling that Bolt was coming. He didn't need to see the fast hip movement or hear the loud yell to know that Bolt was enjoying a happy ending too.

Having almost four hundred pounds of flesh collapsing on top of his vulnerable body took the breath from his chest, and he pushed off the back of the couch with one arm, twisting his body to topple their dead weight onto the carpeting.

He got an elbow in the cheek when he landed on top of the heap of male flesh, but laughed along with the other two. They rolled and continued to laugh as Bolt held his arms down to grasp each of his friend's hands to pull them to their feet. "I don't know what I'd do without the two of you. You know that right?" Clasping their shoulders and leaning over to lay a kiss on each man's lips took longer than the quick contact that he'd intended, but it was also more satisfying for all of them. He sighed, and headed to the bathroom. He needed to get rid of the condom and take a shower. Maybe he would be able to sleep tonight. It had been over a week since he'd slept more than a few hours at a time, and he was feeling the effects of the lack of rest.

Tomorrow promised to be a rough day. He would be entering the family business as the CEO of F & P Industries. His days as the rebel son, who would rather stay away from the home office by traveling and selling their talents to companies that needed what they offered, were over. His parents had started the company with one product and a dream. Now their dream was a multi-million dollar company, and he'd work himself into the grave to keep it going in the right direction.

Bolt knew that something wasn't right about the company's attorneys, but he was confident in Randal's abilities to deal with any legal problems that might be uncovered. Once his mother came out on the healthy side after a bout with breast cancer, his parents had left the business to run itself for weeks at a time, so he knew that he had an uphill battle to look forward to. He should have stepped up before, but hindsight was always the best view. Now he needed to get his shit together and be the man his parents had raised him to be.

Chapter 4

Life wasn't fair, and she knew it. The loud bang of two trays crashing into each other brought her back to the job at hand. She had to pay attention to the computer components that the people on the line had finished and sent ahead for her to inspect.

She checked for sharp tits on the soldered boards, and several other small trouble spots that would cause the boards to be rejected. Her job was important to the company's reputation of being a quality, grade A supplier. Right now, she felt as miserable as she could remember being. So she had to go over everything twice to make certain that she didn't miss something simple.

The dollar menu grease burger and fries for dinner last night had been a big mistake. Her lesson was learned at four o'clock in the morning when she'd puked her guts up on her pillow. It had been a mess, and she'd had to throw away her favorite pillow after an unsuccessful attempt to clean it up. Today in the break room when she'd poured a cup of freshly brewed coffee, she'd had to leave it sitting on the counter while she ran to the trash can to, once again, throw up what little was in her stomach.

If Nicky hadn't handed her a small paper cup of water, she knew she would still be hanging over the trash suffering from dry heaves. To add insult to her misery, Nicky had gently teased her about her hour disappearance on her birthday with the "sexy as fuck" stripper. The "bun in the oven" comment was unnecessary.

Lucy hadn't shared the entire adventure with Nicky; all she'd confessed to was a "quickie" in the office. She'd purposely left hunky, sex god number two out of her story. They'd used a condom; there was no way for her to have gotten pregnant. Well, it was possible, but the odds of her being pregnant from that encounter were pretty slim. It had been two months since that night. She would have felt something off-kilter way before now, right?

She was ready for quitting time, and when the whistle went off, she almost ran to the clock to punch out and hit the road. On the way home, she stopped to get a chocolate shake. She was starving, but didn't want to chance solid foods just yet. She sipped the icy shake cautiously as she drove.

Living twenty miles from work wasn't easy in the winter, but the rent on her little house was very affordable, and since most of the people in the small cul-de-sac were Florida snowbirds, she never had to deal with rowdy neighbors. The worst part of living in the little retirement community was seeing the red flashing lights of the ambulances rushing into the turn-around, ready to gather whatever elderly person that help had been called for in the middle of the night. When her grandparents had died, she'd been allowed to stay in the community because she'd been raised there, and the people knew her. If her lifestyle ever changed, she would be forced to move.

She finished her shake while watching the early evening news.

A late night talk show's canned laughter woke her around midnight, and she stretched before getting up from her comfortable spot on the couch. She grabbed a small slice of the chicken pot pie she'd made two days ago, and moaned as the tender chicken and vegetables slid down her throat, filling the spot that was begging for food. *Good, that's good; it didn't come up, so you don't have to worry about being pregnant.* Not that it would be the end of the world. She actually wouldn't mind having a child of her own. *You don't even know the man's name.*

She could see it now, *"No son, I'm sorry, but your mom was enjoying a one-night stand. All I can tell you about your father is that he was too sexy for me to resist.*

Lucy shook her head as she headed to bed after a shower. Yes, indeed, that was a conversation that she didn't want to have with a child. *Mommy is a floozy.* Seeing her nude figure in the full-length mirror on her closet door, made her sigh. She pulled on cotton panties and an oversized t-shirt to sleep in and went to bed. She had to grin. *Yep, you're a real floozy. Uh huh. I can see it now. I'll need to get a tattoo with Floozy written in the middle of a flower.* Her smile stayed in place as she fell asleep.

The sound of someone pounding on her front door woke her just before her alarm was set to go off. She grabbed a robe from the foot of the bed and went to answer the door. Anne Zimmerman was standing outside dressed in a thin nighty crying.

As Lucy pulled her inside, Anne explained that her lady friend Pauline was dead, and she couldn't help her. The sweet old gal kept repeating herself, while Lucy took the robe from her body, and covered the old lady's thin shoulders.

Anne Zimmerman was a kind old woman that was a pioneer in the LGBT community. She and Pauline had been together for fifty years. If Pauline was dead, Lucy knew that Anne would follow too quickly for the comfort of their children. In her experience with the elderly, couples that were completely devoted to each other like her grandparents had been, and others, such as Anne and Pauline, when one died the other followed; like their heart couldn't beat without the one it still yearned for. Her grandmother had died two weeks after her husband passed; leaving Lucy alone and yet happy that they were together.

She quickly called an ambulance and fixed Anne a hot cup of chamomile tea. "I can call

Joseph and Mary for you if you like." Anne nodded, so Lucy got out her book with friends and their relatives' phone numbers, and made the calls.

Luckily, both of the women's children lived close, so Joseph pulled up right behind the ambulance.

Lucy had to rush to make it to work on time, and punched in with one minute to spare. She wanted a cup of coffee but didn't have time to grab one until her first break. By then she was too thirsty to bother with hot coffee, so she bought a soda and took it back to her station after the break.

Everything went well with work, and she felt pretty good. She had used her lunch break to call Joseph's phone and find out what the situation with Pauline was, and to check in on Anne. She couldn't help but cry as he told her that Pauline had indeed been dead when the EMT's had gotten to her. His mother, Anne, was grieving so hard that the doctor had to give her a sedative, and she would be staying with Mary for a few days. His heartfelt thank you was unnecessary, but she choked out, "You're very welcome, I think the world of both ladies."

It was a good thing that she hadn't had time to apply makeup this morning or she would be sporting the raccoon eye look from the tears she shed over the loss of her neighbor. Why her death bothered Lucy so badly she couldn't understand. This emotional crap was for the birds. Now she had a snotty nose, headache and a sore throat from crying.

Nicky gave her a strange look when they restarted the line, but they were too busy to chat, and Lucy had to pull the new hire aside and speak to her about shoddy soldering. It wasn't her favorite thing to do, but it was part of the job. The girl pouted while Lucy talked, and she shrugged her shoulders.

"You can do the job or not; it's your choice. My job is to make sure every part leaving this line is as perfect as possible. I don't have time to fix mistakes when we are in the middle of a critical order. You were hired to help expedite the product. If you want the job, you have it, but you need to do a better job, or you need to leave."

She started to get up and turned her head toward the door just as a data board slammed into the side of her head. She felt the blood begin to flow down her cheek as her hair was grabbed and her head was slammed onto the inspection table. She heard cursing and screaming, but she was helpless to do anything. The last crack of her head on the desk knocked her out.

She wasn't awake to see the girl being distracted into letting the fistful's of Lucy's hair go long enough to attack Loris Flynn. He was not the kind of man to hit a woman, but he grabbed her and held her back to his front while the police were called, and they waited for them to show up. She was wild, trying to bite his arm, and butting the back of her head against his thick chest. Nicky and one of the other women snagged a leg each and taped them together with nylon reinforced packing tape. It made her a little less dangerous but didn't shut up the filth spewing from her spitting and screaming mouth.

Nicky grinned and began chanting, "I can't hear you, scream louder." She took out one of the squishy earplugs that were protecting her ears from the loud machines in the factory. Holding it in front of the girl and pinching it, enraged the woman. The narrow-eyed look and pursed lips directed her way from the handsome boss made her shiver and lick her lips.

The police rushed in with the paramedics and took control of the situation. Lucy was given a quick assessment and loaded up on the white gurney. Seeing the bloody mess that showed with the mass of blood streaked hair was too much for Nicky. She liked Lucy; the woman was her best friend even if they only met outside of the shop once in a while. Nicky didn't have many friends, and this one, well, she would pray for her. She was no Bible thumper, like her parents, but she believed in prayer.

She looked towards Loris and smiled when the two officers took the crazy girl into custody. He was on her list. So far he had avoided her advances to get him into her life. Maybe now that he'd seen her in action, he would change his mind and accept her offer the next time she asked him to meet her for a drink after work.

She addressed Loris as the paramedics wheeled Lucy out of the office. "Do you mind if I ride along with them, just in case she wakes up and wonders what happened?" She got the hand wave and nod of his head in answer, so she ran to the ladies room to grab her purse from the locker. She didn't have the combination to Lucy's locker, but it was doubtful if the woman would be going home today. She could get her things tomorrow. She ran to the door and hopped into the passenger seat just before the lady medic pulled the back doors closed.

The admitting nurse kept her lips pursed the entire time that Nicky attempted to give them what little information she knew. They were not about to allow her into the cubicle until she answered their questions. She couldn't seem to get the prissy woman to understand that the attack was work-related and that the company would be paying the bills, so Lucy's insurance information was not necessary at this moment.

"Look, just call F & P industries and talk to Loris Flynn, or whoever is in the front offices. They can tell you what you want to know."

She was finally allowed to walk back and sit with her friend. Lucy was still unconscious, but they'd cleaned her face of blood and shaved the side of her head where there was now a three-inch crooked line of stitches. Her left cheekbone was dark purple, and it looked like she was getting a black eye in combination with the rest of her injured face. Nicky took her friend's hand and gave it a squeeze.

"You look like hell, but I'm glad you're alive. We have a birthday to celebrate next month you know; I'm turning twenty-five for the third time. Maybe you'll share the luck this time." She sat in the plastic chair and kept talking for an hour. "I hope the next stripper that we go to see looks at my face first, and not yours. Although, if you look like you do right now when we go, I bet that sexy beast would stalk me instead."

She gave the hand a quick squeeze. "With my luck, he'd be like most wild animals and go for the injured prey. I can't bitch too much; I met a few men that night myself. I have some phone numbers, but haven't had time to call them yet."

She heard what sounded like a herd of people walking towards the cubicle, and watched the curtain swing aside. Her hand went to her mouth to stifle a squeal. If these men were doctors, she was going to slit her wrists so they could stitch her up.

The tall, blonde man filled out his suit like it was made for him. The next man was reading from a notebook, and though, Nicky thought he looked familiar in the face, she didn't know him. That body would be memorable to a woman as small as she was. She had never been with a man that big before. His hair was cut close, but not shaved, and his five o'clock shadow would scrape a woman's skin. Nicky shivered and raised her eyes from his waistband. The suit coat covered anything that might outline his package. She was disappointed, but this wasn't exactly the time or place to troll for men.

The blonde was giving her an exasperated look when she finally looked back at him. She shrugged and grimaced. The big guy ignored her completely. His eyes were focused on Lucy. He walked around the blonde and gently turned Lucy's face sideways, to see her profile. When he focused on her, Nicky gasped at the intense look he gave her.

"You're Nicky?" She nodded, and he smiled.

"Well Nicky, my name is Randal Murphy. I'm the attorney for F&P Industries, and this guy is Bolton Cummings CEO of F&P. We have Loris waiting outside to give you a ride home."

She knew a brush off when it slapped her in the face, no matter how attractive the slapper was. She didn't feel comfortable leaving Lucy vulnerable to two corporate sharks. Especially when they stood to lose a great deal of money if Lucy sued them. It took all of the nerve that she could muster, but she shook her head.

"I'll stay with her. She needs someone who she knows to be here when she wakes up." It was the most reasonable thing she could think to say without accusing them of some imagined wrong that they might do to keep

Lucy from suing the company. "I'm sure you understand, we're friends, and if I've never met you before, it's a good bet that she hasn't met you either. That nut case back at the shop did a number on her, coldcocked her with a data board. Lucy's no wimp, but she hasn't been feeling well for a few days, or she would have mopped the floor with that girl."

Bolt kept his eyes on the real life, Lucy. When he thought of how much time and money they'd spent looking for this woman; hell, just seeing her unmarred profile, he understood why Scott was obsessed. He looked at Randal, "Call Scott."

Randal shook his head and tossed his phone to Bolt. He'd texted Scott the minute he'd realized that their prey was lying right in front of them. "My money says he's here in the next ten minutes."

He looked at Nicky and drew in a deep breath. Loris had asked to follow along so he could give this girl a ride home. From the looks of her and the way she kept trying to look tough and stand by her friend, he could see the attraction for Loris. The man was as dominant as they came, and this little woman fit his type.

He smiled, trying to look harmless. "Nicky, I understand how you're feeling; if my friend was laying there all helpless and vulnerable as Lucy is, I'd be wary too. The thing is, Lucy and I have met once before. It was the night of her birthday a couple of months ago. We met at The Zoo."

He saw her eyes go wide, but they narrowed quickly, and he wondered what she was thinking. "What?"

She was shaking her head and scowling at him. Women didn't scowl at him. They flirted, they simpered, they looked at him with speculation and mental calculators. They didn't give him narrowed eyes or appear to be ready to light into him for some imagined wrong. She had been at The Zoo that evening too; he wanted to know what her problem was.

"Look, Mr. Murphy, I was with her the night of her birthday, and you were not the man she was with." She cocked her head sideways and stared at him for a second. "You were the bartender."

He nodded, at least she remembered that much. "I also met Lucy and Scott in the office. Not that it's any business of yours, but I'm sure she will recognize me if she wakes up while we're here. You can leave, and she'll be fine."

They heard a nurse telling someone that they could not go back there. "Sir, there are too many people in there with the patient now, you'll have to wait for someone to leave."

A man's voice told her to suck it. "That's my woman back there; call a cop if you need to, but I'm going to see her."

Scott came around the corner of the curtain and stopped at the foot of the bed. He didn't bother to talk to anyone, but Lucy's still form and Randal gave Nicky the signal to leave with his thumb.

"Time for you to leave. She's in good hands, and no one will take advantage of her. You have my word." He pulled her to her feet and escorted her from the curtained space. "You don't need to go to work in the morning. Lucy might like it if you visit her tomorrow. If you give me your phone number, I'll make sure someone calls you to let you know how she's doing."

He kept his hand on her bicep all of the way to the vehicle where Loris waited for her. "Here you go, Loris will make sure you get home safely, and if you let him, he might feed you before he drops you off."

He tapped the top of the SUV and went back to his friends, and the woman that had evaded every effort to find her. She was everything that he remembered she had been as far as looks went. When they went back to the office, they would watch the video of the attack to determine what set the female off into such a rage.

He wondered what Bolt had been thinking all of the time they'd been in the room with Lucy. There was no need to speculate on Scott's feelings. All Randal could hope for would be that she matched their first, and only, impression of her, or they were in for some disappointing days ahead.

Chapter 5

For weeks now, Bolt had seen the picture of this woman every day. Scott had haunted the Zoo almost nightly. He'd lost weight and was unreasonable when his friends told him to forget the girl and move on. Randal was half-way in lust with the woman, but Bolt was happy that he hadn't been there that night. If he'd been busy fucking some woman while his parents had died like they had, he would carry that guilt for the rest of his life.

Seeing Lucy lying in the bed today gave him mixed feelings. What if she wasn't open to having three men as lovers? What if she didn't like kids? The questions were many, and the answers were few. He also had to find out what happened today. He had been signing papers for Randal to take over the company's legal business when the normally sedate, Calvin, had rushed in without knocking and told them about the fight inside of the plant.

The gasped words, "blood, cops, ambulance, and lunatic," gave him and Randal reason to run from the front office to the inspection offices that were located near the warehouse. They got there in time to talk to the officers that had a woman shackled and cuffed, lying on the floor. She was still yelling obscenities and attempting to bite anyone within reach.

The cops were trying to figure out the best way to transport her from the floor of the office, out to their squad car. Loris pulled one of the old electric utility trucks near to the door of the office. They loaded her up in the small box on the back of the transport, and one cop sat on his knees, holding her in place while Loris drove them to the parking lot.

Once everyone was back inside, they were apprised of the situation. Loris told them that there should be video feed in the security computers. The name Lucy had caught their attention, and when Loris mentioned that he'd sent Nicky to the hospital with her, Randal had headed for his SUV with Bolt right beside him. The coincidence of the names was too much to ignore. Loris followed Randal's SUV to the hospital.

Knowing that a worker had been attacked in his building made him cringe. He needed to get back and find out who had hired the attacker and why. They were supposed to vet the workers hired at F&P. He would get to the bottom of it, but first, he had to make sure the pretty blonde was going to be alright.

Lucy Posey; the name suited her. Her hair was pale blonde with darker brown streaks, and from the way the sheet flowed over her body, it was obvious that the girl had curves. The shapeless, hospital gown covered her breasts; smashed them down actually, but with breasts the size of hers, perky was not an option.

Her legs began to move up, bending at the knees, as her head tossed sideways. Her bandaged hand lifted to her stomach, and she barely turned from where Bolt stood next to her shoulder, before emptying her stomach's contents all over herself and the clean bedding. She gagged with dry heaves until Randal yelled for the nurse, and Bolt and Scott rolled her onto her side. Tears slid from the corners of her eyes, but the men didn't get the opportunity to see her eyes open. The nurse was joined by another one, and the men were sent to the waiting room. Scott protested, but his complaint was ignored, and Bolt grabbed his wrist and towed him from the cubicle.

"She's not going to get up and run away; this time, we know where to find her, and her address is back in the personnel files at the office."

Scott nodded his head and slumped into one of the plastic chairs near the bank of windows overlooking the canopied emergency entrance. "You're right, it's just been crazy, you know?" He raised his hands and dropped them onto his thighs. "I told myself that I was done. Yesterday I made up my mind that being with her again wasn't meant to be. I've been acting like a crazy man; it's not logical that I'd be so fixated on a one-night stand."

He looked toward the hallway leading back to where Lucy was. "Now I see her again, and even bruised, she's as beautiful as I remember." He shrugged his shoulders.

"What can I say? Stick a fork in me; I'm done?" He sat up straighter when the bossy nurse pointed their way for a man in blue scrubs. "This doesn't look good."

He introduced himself as Doctor Gaines. "The bottom line is, Ms. Posey has a severe concussion, and we've had to remove several small pieces of metal shavings and plastic slivers from her face and head. The dehydration can be attributed to the pregnancy." He took off his glasses and verbally kicked Scott in the gut when he said, "Sadly, she lost the fetus. I'm sorry for her loss, but it is not unusual for an early pregnancy to miscarry due to trauma, whether physical or mental. It happens, and it's no one's fault. She will need to rest for a few weeks to regain her strength.

"The one good thing about this is that she is young and healthy. She woke briefly and knew who she was and what year it is, but fell asleep before we could make any further cognitive determinations." He raised his hand when Scott and Randal began to ask questions.

"We are estimating her to be eight weeks into the pregnancy, but I can see no reason for her to be concerned at this time over any future plans to have a child.

"No, we cannot say when you can take her home, nor can I give you information that we don't have at this time. She's not going anywhere tonight, and we will see how it goes. If she wakes up and is physically able to leave, we'll cut her loose tomorrow. She may need someone to stay with her for a few days, but there is nothing to indicate that she will have further complications."

Scott could only stand there stunned. The doctor had answered his question without knowing that he wanted to know how far along the pregnancy was. He remembered the broken condom and grabbed Bolt's shoulder to hold himself upright. Somehow, someway, something had kept him bird dogging after Lucy all of this time. Fate had a way of stomping on a man's heart when he deserved it.

Randal was staring at him with dawning comprehension. He recalled the sight of the broken condom still hanging from Scott's softening dick, and the cuss words when they'd discussed the odds of this kind of outcome. After that kind of news, there was no way he would leave Scott looking like he'd been shell shocked. He wrapped his arm around the smaller man's shoulders and squeezed.

Bolt had no idea why Scott punched Randal in the gut. As far as he knew, the girl that Scott had tried to bring into the circle had outside interests and had been pregnant. It was time to cut their hopes for her off and move on. He walked to the nurse behind the counter and got the paperwork for her hospital bills taken care of.

She'd gotten injured at work, so the worker's compensation premiums that the company paid for would finally be useful. Once they had all of the information that he could provide, he walked back to the waiting area. Randal sat by himself near the door, and got up, heading for the door without speaking. Bolt followed him to the car and got in.

"So would you like to explain to me what went on back there? While you're at it, where's Scott?"

He rubbed the back of his neck. He had been so busy with work and making plans that he knew he was neglecting the guys. Their friendship had weathered more than a few weeks of negligence before, so this shouldn't be too long or drawn out. He still had to meet with one of the vendors that supplied miniature screws for some of the delicate panels that the company specialized in. Once Randal began the tale of Scott and Lucy, Bolt closed his eyes and tried to picture events as Randal told them.

"So this instant lust thing actually happened?"

Randal nodded as he made the turn from the parking lot. "Oh yeah, he was hard as a rock right on stage, and I'd swear that the juice was dripping down her legs. I ended up turning off the stage lights just to get them off of the platform. By the time I got Jesse and Calvin up onstage to finish Scott's set, his face was buried in her snatch, and she was clawing the shit out of his shoulders. She was as wild as he was, and seeing them like that made me hard. You haven't seen the girl's eyes, but trust me, clouded with lust they look damn inspiring. I offered her my cock, and after a very slight hesitation, she latched on and sucked me dry."

"After Scott ran out to take care of the fight between a bunch of women, Lucy acted a little embarrassed, but not ashamed." He shrugged his wide shoulders, "She's adorable, and I believe I told her at the time that I wished I'd seen her first."

Bolt groaned and clasped his hands in his lap. From the tone of his voice, Randal was almost as fixated as Scott. Something had to be special about the girl that he hadn't seen so far. Maybe he'd make time tomorrow and try to discover the attraction, well, aside from her physical appearance. They'd all fucked beautiful women, not so beautiful women, and even more than one woman at the same time. They'd enjoyed life without becoming attached to any one female, now it seemed that two of their group might have found that elusive "One and only."

"So I assume that Scott or you, or both of you forgot to suit up before diving in?" He couldn't believe that the important rule of condoms had been forgotten, the girl couldn't be that good. Could she? "How do you figure its Scott's responsibility? If she'd screw with two strangers like that, what makes you think she doesn't make a habit of having sex with whoever she's attracted to?" He saw Randal's lips tighten, and his jaw clench. "Look, I'm not trying to insult her or the two of you. From what I saw, she's a beautiful girl with a nice figure. I can't believe that she's so damn perfect. If she is then we have a few problems."

Randal unclenched his teeth. Getting pissed at Bolt would do no good. "Scott wore a condom; it broke. I saw it, he saw it, and she was swallowing my cock at the time, so it's doubtful that she knew or would have remembered. I told you, she was as hot as we were. We were lucky that we all finished before the cat fight started in the bar.

"Afterward, she was pretty rattled. She mumbled about celebrating her birthday, and how Karma was paying her back for laughing at some guy at work." Randal smiled at the memory of Lucy trying, and then giving up being modest as she got dressed. "She left before I could get more than her name. Scott was ready to kick my ass when he got back, and she was gone."

He filled in the rest of the story, ending with, "I keep seeing those eyes when I close my eyes. I'm damned near as crazy about her as Scott, and I'm not dealing with that fact very well. I don't lose my mind over any woman or a random piece of ass. This woman, I want her." Bolt didn't know what to say.

They got back to the office and went straight to the security cabinet. By the time they'd finished watching the footage from the inspection office, Bolt knew what Randal had meant by the girl's eyes being fascinating. The still pictures of her didn't show the jeweled blue color of her eyes, or the animation in her face as she spoke. She had wide lips that appeared to pout even as they rested closed while she tried to deal with the younger woman. Her mistake had been in turning away from the mentally challenged girl.

The vendor was waiting for him when he finally got to his office, and work took his thoughts for the rest of the afternoon. Randal left him to deal with his own business for the company. Of all the days that crazy things could have happened on, this appeared to be the day that fate decided to play hell and havoc with.

The vendor wanted to deal with the former vice president; the one that had left as soon as he was told that Bolt would be taking the reins himself. If he wanted to deal with Jenkins, then he could take his happy ass down the road, and Bolt would be happy to find another supplier. Once he'd established his determination to negotiate on his own behalf, the cocky bastard dropped his self-importance and decided to keep the contract that he'd come for.

Once the contracts were signed, and the man left the building, Bolt cleared his desk and locked the drawers before leaving for home. He had a great deal to think about from the day's happenings.

Chapter 6

Lucy heard herself groan before she opened her eyes. Blast it, her head hurt like crazy, and when she tried to raise her hand to the side of her head, she couldn't move it. Someone had her hand entwined in theirs, and if the size was any indication, it wasn't a woman's hand. She opened her eyes slowly. Thankfully it was dim in the room, but the light still hurt her eyes.

She could see that she was lying in a hospital bed, and when she looked down to her lap, a man's shaggy head lay on her leg, and her hand was held in his hand close to his lips.

She gasped. It was the stripper from her birthday. He sported a heavy two or three-day-old beard and mustache, but he was as sexy with clothing on as he was without. *Almost, Lucy; he's almost as sexy.* How did he find her, and what was he doing here? For that matter, what was she doing here?

She closed her eyes because her head was beginning to pound with every breath. She couldn't help it, she cried out and squeezed his hand as hard as she could to help deal with the pain in her head. She could feel the tears running down her face, and when the nausea hit, she was helpless to stop in time to run into the bathroom or anywhere else for that matter. She vomited on herself and barely heard the masculine voice berating the nurse for allowing *his* Lucy to be sick and in so much pain.

The next time she woke, she heard masculine voices speaking quietly. Her head still throbbed, but not to the point of nausea. Her stomach was sore from straining to throw up contents that hadn't been there, and she was so thirsty that she could barely swallow past the dryness of her throat. She let her eyes open in slits to begin with. Since the pain behind her eyes didn't intensify, she opened them more, until she could see the room that she was lying in.

Her first thought upon seeing the three men sitting at a small table near the foot of her bed was, wow. Nicky would be in hog heaven amidst these guys. Her stripper was there, and looking at the dark haired giant with the wicked blue eyes, she remembered his taste. She closed her eyes quickly as she remembered that night.

Were these guys haunting her for some reason? Did she die and this was her psyche's idea of heaven? If it was, how come she'd added another man? That red head was fine too, from what she could see. She peeked at the men again to make sure that she actually did see three men.

Yep, there they are; and since when did you fantasize about men in three piece suits? Not that they weren't sexy, they looked too good; that's all. Too put together. Even her stripper wore a suit; though his didn't have a necktie, but he wore a suit coat and slacks.

She left her eyes on them and scooted up as she pressed the button on the handrail to make the head of the bed rise. She knew that the noise startled the men, but screw it, playing possum was not in her DNA. She preferred to take situations head on. It saved a lot of worry and second guessing herself. Right now she wished she was a bit of a coward.

"Hello, I seem to have dropped into the rabbit hole or something. I hope you can pardon me for my sketchy memory here, but why am I lying in this bed, and why are you here? By the way, would you please hand me that cup of water? I'm dying of thirst, and it's too far away for me to reach."

The redhead brought the water to her and held it close enough for her to suck the straw between her lips. She drank several long pulls of the icy cold water before sitting back and nodding in thanks to the green-eyed man that wore a small, sexy smile. "Thank you." She turned her head to look at the other two men.

"I'm puzzled; though I hate to admit this, I have no idea what your names are. I don't suppose you can tell me how you found me here? As far as I know, we didn't exchange names or anything that night, or am I not remembering something I should?"

She raised her hand to check out the side of her head that felt weird. "Oh, my, God. What happened to me? Someone shaved my head." Her voice got higher with each word that she spoke. She felt the stitches and drew her fingers down to look at them as if the imprint of the stitches were there for her to examine. She felt lost and a little afraid too. What had she done? She was a little clumsy at times, but everyone went through balance issues at times. From the looks she was getting from the men, she hoped they didn't plan to treat her like a mindless child.

Red stayed next to her and offered her another drink, and she took a quick swallow before he started talking.

"My name is Bolton Cummings; I own F&P Industries. You were attacked by another woman that you had given a verbal warning to for shoddy work. When you turned away, she cold cocked you with a data board. If it's any consolation, you didn't stand a chance." He gestured toward her head. "I'm sorry about your hair and the injuries, but the company will take care of the bills, and you will receive worker's compensation for the days you've missed from the job.

"As for the why; her name is Jordan Tuttlemen, and she used her sister's identification to get the job at F&P. She actually has a history of violence and knew that she would never have gotten hired under her own name." He smoothed the sheet covering her torso and looked over to the other men in the room.

"Randal Murphy is the big guy. He is my attorney. The beach bum there is Scott Henderson. He is a business partner in other dealings, like The Zoo. As to how they found you? Well, it was by accident. Randal and I recognized your name and Nicky's, and once we got a good look at you, we called Scott. You've been a hard woman to find."

Scott was on her other side, and he was gazing at her like she was a steak dinner or something. One of his hands rested on her stomach, and she shifted to dislodge it. He placed the hand right back when she settled down. She frowned and took her time eyeing each man.

Bolton looked at her with what she considered amused concern, and Randal had a smile on his lips, hell, even his eyes were smiling. Scott kept his eyes on her face, but the hunger she sensed was a bit unsettling.

"Look, I think it's really nice of you all to be concerned, but I don't know what to tell you." Her stomach decided to voice its opinion of the lack of food, and she smiled. "As you can hear, the big growls are eating the little growls because my stomach is empty. I'm going to call a nurse or someone to scare up a meal or crackers or something for me. I'll be fine, and it was nice meeting you all." She reached for the call button without looking down, because these men were beginning to scare her a little. She left her finger on the pressure pad, pressing two different buttons at the same time. Nothing happened to the bed, so her hopes of calling a nurse increased.

Scott didn't appreciate the way she dismissed him. Like she had no regard for the father of her baby, or maybe Bolt was right to be skeptical. Maybe she had a man on the side that no one knew about. He couldn't resist asking her, "When we met, you told me that you didn't have a significant other in your life; do you want us to call anyone special to come up here to be with you?" He hated to think that there might be someone in her life, but he wanted to get to the truth of her relationship status.

Bolt narrowed his eyes at her, and she wondered why the man suddenly seemed hostile. She hadn't done anything wrong, so she scowled back at him. "I don't understand any of this, well not much of it anyway. It must be the blow to my head. I need food, and then I need to sleep. Hopefully, by morning, I'll be able to comprehend everything, and answer any questions that I need to." There, she'd been nice, even though she was beginning to feel worse with each passing minute. She rolled her aching head toward Scott and Randal, "There's no one; when I told you he left me for his neighbor, it was the truth."

Scott picked up her left hand and checked out the ring finger. There were no tell-tale signs of a ring indent, or even an older curve in the lower third of the finger. He came to the conclusion that the past relationship had not been serious enough for the man to put a visible claim on her. It gave him a good feeling, why? *Does it matter? She's free, and she didn't lie.* He could tell that she was beginning to panic from the way she seemed to pull back and gather the covers tighter around her body. He patted her leg and backed away from the side of the bed. "Why don't we let you get some rest for now and on our way out, we'll ask the nurse to bring you something to eat. I can imagine that you're tired of all the talking for now."

He couldn't stop himself from stepping close again and bending down to place a tender kiss on her cheek next to her lips. "Later." He turned and walked out of the room. It was against his nature to walk away from her now that he'd found her, but he would be back. Hopefully, she would be more willing to talk then.

Two nurses were at the desk when he approached, and their reaction to seeing him standing there in front of the station was familiar. He was pretty sure that they knew him from the bars that he and his partners owned. He was the partner that was most visible to the public. They were very helpful, smiling and playing with their hair, and they went into immediate action via a phone call to the kitchen, when he requested that they find something to eat for Lucy Posey. He grinned and shook each woman's hand in thanks for doing him a favor. He reached into the inside pocket of his suitcoat and produced two passes for a table and VIP status at The Zoo.

"I know how hard you angels work; I hope you will accept these for a night out to relax and have a good time. Lucy is important to me, and this is the only way I have right now to thank you for taking such good care of her." He gave them another smile and walked to the elevator. He had a lot to plan out and hoped that his Lucy was open to an unusual living arrangement.

The pregnancy had been a surprise, but he was now convinced that he'd been pushed by fate to find her after that night. He could barely comprehend the reason for the ache in his chest when he realized that the child was lost. When the doctor said pregnant, his heart had plummeted, then jacked up thinking that his broken condom was a mixed blessing. The immediate news of the loss of the child gave him the strangest need to find Lucy and hold her tight. It didn't matter to him who the father of the baby was, the child was his, even if it had only been for a few seconds.

His own father had been so busy working to feed and house his family that he was wiped out by the time he got home from the job. He tried to listen to each kid for at least a few hours a week, but more often than not, Vince Henderson fell asleep on the couch, as he watched the evening news.

The old man took his last nap on the new floral couch that Scott had bought for his mother's birthday. His mother treasured the now ragged, broken down thing to this day. He'd tried to replace it, but Mom told him no, so he didn't push. Why he was thinking about them tonight puzzled him for a few seconds.

His mother would have been tickled to death to know that he would be presenting her with a new grandbaby to bake cookies with. It didn't seem to matter how many babies toddled through the old doublewide; she had room in her heart for all of them. Knowing that he needed to visit soon occupied his mind while he rode the elevator down to the hall leading to the parking garage.

For a man that rarely thought about future children with any enthusiasm, he was damn sure happy about the possibility of a child of his own. The loss of that child was a kick in the gut.

He was happy that the night was clear. He mounted up on the old bike. His oldest brother had passed the cycle down to him when Ivan went into the service. Tonight was perfect for a ride, and there was nothing better to clear his thoughts than feeling the freedom of the wind hitting his body at eighty miles an hour running down the highway. He knew that Bolt and Randal would be waiting to talk to him, but tonight he needed some space and time to sort himself out.

Randal walked over to the large window and checked his messages while Bolt tried to make small talk with Lucy.

One of the nurses that had shown them to Lucy's room brought a plastic wrapped plate into the room and set it down on the small bed table.

"How are you feeling tonight, honey? Let's get this bed straightened out and make you a little more comfortable. I imagine that it's time for a trip to the restroom too." She smiled at Lucy and patted her arm where it lay on the wrinkled mess of covers.

She looked at the men in turn with a raised eyebrow. "It's after visiting hours, so please say your goodbyes. Ms. Posey needs to get cleaned up, and I need to assess her condition, so please make it quick." Her smile was friendly but showed no interest in furthering conversation with the men.

Randal scowled at both women but defiantly leaned down to give Lucy a quick kiss on top of her head. He added, "I'll be back tomorrow; you're in good hands with us, kitten." He winked and headed for the door while Bolt raised his eyes heavenward.

"You know, we need to talk, but I can understand that you need privacy and time to heal." He came close and picked up her right hand. The nails were short, and the calluses on the pads of her fingers received a tender rub from his thumb. "Dream well, Ms. Posey; I'll see you in a day or two." He kissed the back of the hand that he still held, placed it back on her leg, and left the room.

The nurse and Lucy watched the handsome men meet in the hallway before the door closed, and their view was gone.

"Honey, I don't know what it is that you have, but I want some of it. In fact, every nurse under fifty wants to know how you got those three to mother hen you the way they have been since you came in yesterday afternoon." She pulled the blankets back and helped Lucy swing her legs over the side of the bed to dangle for a few minutes. She went to the wardrobe and brought back a clean hospital gown.

"Let's get you in the bathroom, and once you use the toilet, how about a nice shower?"

The trip to the bathroom was the longest ten feet that Lucy could remember walking in her lifetime. It was a good thing that Nurse Rhonda was there with a strong arm to help her keep upright on the way. Having her help her sit on the stool was embarrassing, but her blushes were wasted on the older woman. Nurse Rhonda was getting the water for her shower up to temperature.

Lucy used the grab bar to pull herself to a standing position, but needed Nurse Rhonda to steady her into the shower and sitting down on the shower bench.

"Look, I understand that you are independent and all that stuff, but trust me, I've seen it all before, in various sizes and shapes." She chuckled and shook her head as she rinsed the shampoo from Lucy's hair. "One time I had a woman that hated water. She screamed bloody blue murder when I got her all wet. It turned out that she was afraid of drowning. I imagine someone could drown in a shower; it would be hard to do, but if your mind was made up to it, I guess anything is possible." She soaped a washcloth and handed it to Lucy to clean the "important parts."

With the chatter from Nurse Rhonda, embarrassment was forgotten, and the shower actually gave her a pick me up. Now if she could get that sandwich down her throat to make her stomach quit burning, she might get closer to feeling human. She snatched the plastic covered plate as they toddled past the table, and lowered her into the plastic chair. She was so intent on the dry bread; she didn't notice the carry-out bag sitting on the bed.

Nurse Rhonda laughed at the way Lucy was fixated on the food in her hand. She dropped the sack on her lap and turned back to strip the bed.

There was a small chocolate shake and a cheeseburger and fries in the sack. It left Lucy with the task of what to do with the cold sandwich that the nurse had so thoughtfully brought. That cheeseburger had her name on it, and the first sip of the shake gave her cause to moan in pleasure. She dropped the sandwich back into the plastic and set it aside as she filled her cheeks with beef and fries.

There was nothing delicate or mannerly about the way that meal disappeared; even the deep belch after the wrappers had been tossed into the trash was unapologetic. Lucy sat back in the chair and sighed. "I was so hungry that I made a pig of myself, but I needed that meal." She sucked the last drops of chocolate from the plastic cup. "I don't actually know those guys well, but with service like this, a girl could get used to them."

Nurse Rhonda grinned and nodded in agreement. "I could spend hours just staring at them. Especially Scott. Now that man would make a hooker blush. Most of the nurses have seen him at The Zoo. You know he's sexy as can be in clothes, but without them, he is gorgeous. Even Miss Fiona thinks he is a 'fine specimen of manhood.'" The nurse held up her fingers on each hand to make quotation marks for the words of praise from the absent Fiona. "She has been stalking him, but he doesn't date the patrons, as he's told her so several times. She thinks he will stop playing hard to get sooner or later, but after talking to him tonight, I'm not so sure."

She fluffed the bed pillows and pulled the covers back for Lucy to get in. She offered her hand, and Lucy didn't bother protesting or trying to make the few steps on her own. Her head was not as fuzzy as it had been, but she wanted to close her eyes for a few minutes because the lids felt so heavy. She laid back on the pillows and fell asleep while Nurse Rhonda took her blood pressure.

Morning brought several vases of flowers. The biggest potted Peace Lily that she'd ever seen arrived around ten in the morning after the cut flowers and the card on the lily was from F&P Industries. A large box of chocolates from the expensive candy store in the mall showed up just before lunch was served.

Lucy shared her goodies with the nurse's aide and the cleaning lady. They seemed surprised, but bit into the candies with as much enthusiasm as Lucy did. The aide was gifted with a carnation for her hair, for helping her get to the bathroom.

By noon, she was ready to leave. She was waiting for the doctor to show up to spring her but realized that her clothing was filthy. The shirt was splattered with blood and factory dust from the grinders and filings. She asked the nurse if she could borrow a set of scrubs, but never got an answer.

****

Scott showed up before the doctor, and she didn't know what to say to him. It was an awkward situation. "Look, I don't understand why you're here. Every nurse in the place has been in here today asking when you would be visiting again."

Challenging him might not be the smartest thing for her to do, but she was tired of fielding questions about their relationship. She really resented the fact that her pulse sped up when the man was in her sight. There was no blaming the alcohol on her attraction to him this time. No, it was all natural, and remembering him in his "all natural" state made her blush. If she had been wearing panties when he turned that sexy smile towards her like he just did, they would be soaked, and she resented knowing that she had so little self-control.

The tightening of those sexy lips and narrowed eyes told her that she'd finally penetrated his good humor. His head tilted sideways and just as he opened his mouth to talk, the doctor walked in.

He was looking at the chart in his hands and almost ran into the foot of the bed before he looked up and smiled at Lucy. "Hi, Lucy. I see that you kept your breakfast down this morning. Now, I am going to let you go home today, but you need to make an appointment with your gynecologist as soon as possible."

He took her wrist between his fingers and consulted his watch before pulling the covers back and pressing on her lower tummy. "You need to take your vitamins, at least for a few weeks, and make sure you get plenty of rest." He patted her shoulder and turned her shocked face towards the door so he could see the sewn up wound. "You need to try to stay out of fights like the one that caused this. You were fortunate that you were in the hospital when you miscarried; everything checked out fine, and you will be able to be back to normal in a week or two."

He checked her eyes with his penlight and touched her bruising while she flinched. "I'm sorry this hurts; I'm trying to be gentle. I understand that you want to leave. I don't see a problem with that as long as you have someone to stay with you for a few days. You have a concussion; just because your head isn't pounding, doesn't mean that the skull has healed so fast."

Scott stood up and walked closer to the bed. The doctor nodded when he saw Scott take Lucy's hand.

"I see that you have adequate companionship, so I'll get those papers ready when I finish my rounds in this hallway." He patted her again and turned to Scott. "Watch her for dizziness, and nausea, or excessive bleeding. With the miscarriage, she might become emotional over just about anything, so if she gets cranky or starts to cry for no reason, you need to remember that her hormones are driving her actions." He wagged his finger under the younger man's nose. "If she irritates you, suck it up. Be a man and make sure she knows she's loved. Too many women don't get that from their men." His head wagged back and forth as he walked to the door. "Damn fools, if she loves you enough to have your baby, you can love her enough to understand it that takes a lot out of a woman when she loses a baby; one month or five, it doesn't matter. She will need you to be there." He waved his hand absently as he walked through the doorway.

Scott still held her hand in his. Lucy looked at her hand that laid over her stomach. Her mouth was halfway opened, but she hadn't uttered a sound since the doctor had begun talking.

He had a bad feeling seeing the panicked look in her eyes. "I'm going to go out on a limb here and speculate that you had no idea that you were pregnant?" Her eyes raised to look at him. He could see that she was indeed shocked. *Oh hell.* No wonder she hadn't figured it out before now.

"We need to talk, but how about I take you home, and we can spend a few days together and straighten everything out. Do you think we can do that?" The caution entering her expressive face made him scramble for words to keep her from screaming at him. "I promise, no fooling around unless you want to. I know that it might not seem like it, but I do have control over my actions." He kept his hold on her hand and raised it to his lips. "What do you say? I'll even give you time to yell at me for the broken condom."

Nurse Fiona waltzed into the room, and the noise of the door latch snapping shut woke Lucy from her stupor. The nurse was gorgeous, but Scott continued to hold onto her hand and smile tenderly at her. Even when the jealous woman sidled up close next to Scott's side while she lowered the bed rail. Lucy had met the woman before breakfast but hadn't seen her again until now. Recalling Nurse Rhonda's gossip from last night made her look at the beautiful nurse.

"Will I be allowed to borrow a set of scrubs to go home in? I can wash them and bring them back in a few days, as soon as I get my car from work."

Scott shook his head and walked over to the chair that he'd been sitting in when he came into the room. "I brought you something to wear to go home in, sweetheart. Don't worry, I charged it to Bolt's card, so you can think of it as a replacement for the clothes that were ruined when you were hurt." His grin invited her to smile, and whether it was to needle the confident Fiona or genuine happiness for his thoughtfulness, she didn't know, but she gave him a small smile of thanks.

"That's great, now if you don't mind, you need to wait in the hallway while this pretty nurse helps me dress, then I'll let you take me home." He grinned and walked to the door. The scowling nurse helped her pull the hospital gown from her shoulders and dumped the bag containing a pair of shorts and a pretty, baby blue tank top with a short sleeved, cotton button up shirt to wear over the set. Lucy wondered how he knew her sizes, and laughed when she saw the garish flip flops decorated with giant flowers.

Her old clothes were in a clear bag hanging in the small closet, and Nurse Fiona called an aide to push a cart full of flowers and the Peace Lily down to the front entrance where Scott had run ahead and pulled his sports car around to pick her up. The flowers had their water dumped right on the pavement because he wasn't about to allow liquid to possibly spill on the expensive interior of his "baby."

He cursed the large plant but adjusted his attitude when he saw the hurt look on Lucy's face, and the smug smile on the nurse's face. "It's okay, sweet; we can put the flowers in water when we get them home." He leaned down and pulled her from the wheelchair and gave her a hug. "How about I phone ahead and we can stop in at The Zoo so I can run in and grab dinner?" Lucy nodded at the same time he helped her to get comfortable in the seat of the low slung vehicle.

"I'm not helpless, Scott; I can manage to put on a seatbelt you know."

His answer warmed her too much. "I know that. I don't consider you helpless, sweet; I consider you precious, big difference." He kissed the top of her head and stood back enough to shut the door. That smug look was gone from Fiona's face when he turned to go around the car to the driver's side. The woman actually looked like she might cry. He nodded toward her and said, "Thank you." She was still standing there as they drove away.

Chapter 8

All the way to The Zoo, Lucy stayed quiet. She kept closing her eyes and opening them to see if she had dreamt the past two hours. *Nope, you're still sitting in a car that cost more than you make in five years at the factory. Face it; you are wide awake, and let's not forget that little bun in the oven thing either.*

She groaned at that phrase. It was the same one that Nicky had teased the hell out of her with. "A broken condom." She tossed her hand up in the air and shook her head. "That's what happens when you let Nicky talk you into going out. *Let's have fun*, she said; *Let's cut loose*, she said."

She didn't realize that she was talking to herself out loud, but Scott heard every word, and he wasn't about to shut her up. Her mind worked over time. He recognized the signs because he used to do the same thing. Of course, that was when he was still in grade school, but it helped him to get his thoughts organized. He hated to stop the car, but they were at The Zoo, and their food would be waiting for him to pick it up. He parked the car, and Lucy dropped her hands onto her lap.

When she looked up at him, she asked, "Can you bring me one of those shakes again? I really enjoyed the last one." He grinned and nodded.

"One large, chocolate malted milkshake coming up. Sit tight; I'll be right back, okay?" Her nod was answer enough for him.

He locked the doors from his door panel and hurried across the parking lot to enter the bar. By the time he returned, he saw that his companion had fallen asleep. He hadn't been gone ten minutes, but she had a pretty nasty concussion. He keyed the lock and set the food on top of the car while he opened the door, bending inside to arrange a spot amidst the flowers for their food.

Lucy was sitting up and yawning. As much as he hated to do it, he handed her the large, Styrofoam cup and a straw once he got ready to drive them to her place. No one had ever been allowed to eat or drink in his vehicle before, and it made him shake his head at his actions. He had to ask where she lived as she sipped the drink. Instead of answering him right away she asked him to stop at the factory so she could get her purse.

"My keys are in my purse. My car is alright in the parking lot for a day or two, but I need keys to get inside my house. I don't have a second set of keys hidden around outside like a lot of my neighbors do. I live in a senior community, at least for now. I got grandfathered in when my grandparents passed away. They raised me, so I was there before the street voted to become over fifty occupancy only. It's perfectly legal, you know.

Scott grinned as she kept talking. The one thing that was for certain, he was correct when he thought that she was processing and arranging the thoughts running rampant through her mind. To someone who didn't know better, they might think that she was randomly picking out subjects to talk about. He knew better. She might have a touch of ADD, but his money said that her brain was busily sorting information.

Bolt brought her purse out to the parking lot himself. Scott told him that he would call later tonight after he got Lucy settled, and he nodded and walked back inside the building.

Lucy felt kind of sorry for the big red haired man. "He looks so lonely; like he's got the world on his shoulders or something." She kept her eyes on his figure until the car turned away. "I felt sorry for him when I saw the news about the plane crash. They said that he was their only child. It isn't easy when you are the only one left in a family. When my grandparents died, I was lost for a while."

Twenty minutes later they pulled into the driveway of her small home. She warmed up the food while Scott brought her flowers inside.

"Hey, Lucy? There's a lady with a cane standing out here, and she wants to make sure I'm not moving in or keeping you hostage or something."

Lucy held onto the furniture and then the door jamb until she got to the doorway. "Oh hi, Miss Eloise. I'd like you to meet Scott

Henderson. He's a good friend and will be staying with me for a day or two. I had an accident, and he has been sweet enough to offer to stay and help me if I need it." The old woman grinned and raised her eyebrows.

"Sure, Lucy. I just wanted to make sure you were alright; one can't be too careful nowadays you know." She moved in for a hug, and whispered, "This one looks like a keeper, girlie." She drew back and eyed Scott's backside as he hauled the big lily into the cottage.

Lucy smiled and nodded, "You know it. I'm lucky to have so many caring friends and neighbors. Thank you."

Eloise sent her a thumbs up as she continued her daily patrol of the street.

Scott had rescued their meal from the microwave, so she joined him at the small kitchen table and dug into the delicious cheeseburger and fries. The fries were slightly soggy from being in a sack and then reheated, but they still tasted great.

He was scarfing his meal faster than she was hers, and when he got the hiccups, she laughed.

"That's what you get for inhaling your food. You can slow down; I'm hungry, but I think I have enough food in front of me that I won't have to steal yours." The small belch that snuck out of her mouth gave both of them a reason to laugh, and she murmured, "Excuse me," but didn't let the breach in manners stop her from finishing her meal.

Once the greasy food was consumed and all evidence except the wrappers in the trash was gone, Scott insisted that Lucy needed a nap.

"I know you're tough and all. Please look at it my way. You just got out of the hospital, and you just lost our baby. I'm not trying to make you feel bad, but I have a sister that has four kids, and I remember how tired she always was."

He was getting on her nerves. Yes, she was tired, but she wasn't used to someone telling her what she should do and what she shouldn't. The arrogant way he declared that she'd miscarried his baby, that bugged her. It made her wonder how he found out to begin with.

She had briefly considered the possibility of pregnancy when she began getting sick to her stomach at odd times. Her periods were almost always screwed up, so the few short spotty days of her cycles were not cause for alarm. Knowing that they'd used a condom, and since it was a one-time thing, the odds were slim to none for pregnancy.

The thing that bothered her was his certainty that the baby was his, she could have had a lover. She didn't, but- *You dingbat, you told him there was no one else; you might as well pat him on the back and tell him how manly he is for knocking your ass up.* She was not about to take him on as her keeper.

She headed to the small living room and sat down in the corner of the couch. She turned her body towards him when he sat close, but not crowding her.

"Look, I need some time to let this pregnancy thing sink in. I went to the bar with Nicky that night because it was my twenty-eighth birthday. I usually go see a movie, or stop and buy a steak to broil for dinner to celebrate." She allowed her eyes to rise and look into his briefly but immediately dropped her eyelids. The overwhelming attraction was still there.

He was gorgeous and made her want to pull the shirt from his shoulders and lick his smooth skin. "I want to know how you found out that I was in the hospital, and- " She gestured towards him with her hand. "Just start at the beginning, please. I remember the attack at work; well, part of it anyway. I can understand how Bolton Cummings got involved, although I'm surprised that he didn't send that ass Lee Snooker from Human Resources to deal with the hospital."

"As for that night; I have a perfect recollection, so we don't need to rehash it." She groaned the last few words, because he had pulled her feet up onto his lap, and begun rubbing her toes and instep.

He knew that she could feel the way his cock was reacting to the feel of her foot lying over the top of where it laid along his upper thigh, but he kept his hold on her foot in his hands. He wasn't crazy enough to try to do something about the hard on she was inspiring. Telling himself that he was a sick son of a bitch for even thinking about sex the minute she got out of the hospital, didn't change things much.

"Okay, let's see; that night, when I got back to the office, you were gone. I almost punched Randal for not stopping you, or at least, getting your number. I understand that you might find it hard to believe, but I don't connect with women like I connected with you that night." He rubbed the ball of her foot and she closed her eyes and hissed through her teeth. Her foot jerked in his hold but stayed between his hands. "We looked through the charge slips, the video feeds, hell, I grilled every person in the place. No one knew you." He set her foot down on his thigh and picked up the other one to give it a massage too.

"I've spent weeks canvassing the local watering holes and fast food places with no success in my attempts to find you. Hiding out here in the suburbs is the last place I thought to look. Randal has been with me every step of the way, and we roped Bolt into the search too." He ran his hand up to her calf and gently massaged the tight muscle.

"I had decided to give up the search because you were becoming an obsession for me. Like I said, that connection that we have every time we see each other- No, don't shake your head. At least be truthful here." He saw her head shake to deny his words, but he could see the flush on her cheeks and feel the way her breath sped up while he rubbed her soft skin. She wouldn't look at him because she knew that he would mirror back to her the same look that she felt.

"Go ahead; tell me that you don't feel the heat. I dare you to lie about it. Don't you know how incredibly rare something like this is?" Her head flopped back on the high armrest of the couch. She was fighting it, but he could understand that. He decided to finish his explanation.

"So, I was at the bar on Cleveland when I get a call and a text from Randal. He said that Bolt had found you. Up until then we only had your first name and knew that your birthday was on the twenty-eighth." I left the bar and rode to the hospital on the bike. Even though Randal assured me that it was you, I had to see you for myself."

Her eyes were open, and she stared at him for several seconds. "No one has ever affected me like you do. As for your friend Randal, he's another story. I wanted him; I'm not going to lie to you. I don't know what came over me. I've been wondering what kind of woman would feel such need to have two men at one time like that. I'm sorry, but it doesn't matter how I look at it. I should be ashamed of my behavior that night." She reached her hand out and touched Scott's jaw. "You've been truthful with me; I'm going to be truthful with you here. I should be ashamed, but I'm not. If the opportunity came along again, I'm not sure I would even try to resist the temptation."

"You need to see this from my point of view. I went out for some fun. I got more than I ever imagined that I would want or enjoy." She smiled with a little twist of her full lips. "I've never acted like that in my life, but there you were. I went home and thought my actions would haunt me all night, or that I would never look at myself in the mirror with any dignity again." Her blue eyes held the sheen of tears, but nothing was falling from them yet. She was proud of her ability to hold them from falling down her cheeks. The lump in her throat was hard to talk around, but she cleared it away and said, "I wasn't ashamed, but I wasn't happy with my actions either. I couldn't blame it on the alcohol. I'd had two drinks, and let me tell you, the bartenders at The Zoo are cheap with your booze."

She dropped her feet to the floor and pushed herself up to a sitting position and stood from there. "I need to get some sleep, so help yourself to the extra blankets in the spare bedroom closet. I don't keep the sheets on the bed because no one ever stays over. I don't have much in the fridge, but you are welcome to whatever you can find to eat. I need to go to the store tomorrow and buy groceries." She didn't say another word, just turned towards the short hallway where the bathroom and bedrooms were located.

Scott sat on the couch where she'd abandoned him. He couldn't help but grin from her revelations of non-guilt. She probably thought that he would have a problem with her confession about liking the ménage sexual encounter. He had to make a few calls and straighten out his schedule for the next few days, and then there was the matter of how to gain her cooperation in possibly moving in with three men.

Bolt was looking at houses; how serious he was about finding a home was in question, but maybe it was time for a heart to heart with the men that he loved more than his own life.

Scott had been spending the past three days with Lucy, and that arrangement would have to be addressed at some point very soon too. Randal was the only one of the three of them that seemed to act normal, except Bolt noticed the concern in his eyes each time he looked his way. The men had never allowed anything to come between them before, and Bolt refused to let the collective stress become a reason to divide them.

He called the meeting, avoiding an argument with Scott by telling him the meeting would be quick. Scott came in first and grabbed a beer from the fridge. "I need this; she's driving me up the damn wall." He drank the bottle within minutes and went back for another one. This time, the beer sat in his hand for a while before he started sipping on it.

"I'm ready to scream and pull out my hair. Did you know that she can take care of herself; she doesn't need a man?" He pointed the bottle towards Bolt and grumbled. "According to her, I shouldn't worry about her; she has a job and insurance, so she really doesn't need me or anyone else for that matter." He stomped into the living room and sat down on the edge of the sofa.

"So, I'm an unnecessary person in her life right now, and I'm told that I should go back to the bar and drive the *'chickie's'* into sexual frenzies so that they will throw money at me. She says that I distract her and that even though she's attracted to me, it doesn't mean anything." He pointed at Bolt and jabbed his finger for emphasis. The door opened and distracted him for a minute; he shook his head and pointed towards Randal, who had just come in.

"She says that she can't make a life with me because you and I ruined her for just one man. She says that she enjoyed the experience with the two of us that night so much, that she couldn't promise to stick with me alone." He lowered his head as he sat with his legs spread and elbows on his knees. The beer bottle was being rolled between his hands, and Scott looked almost defeated.

"She told me that she isn't a liar and won't start telling lies now, but I don't know if she's trying to scare me off with that confession, or if she actually means it. I should be happy that she likes it with more than one partner, but is what she says real?"

Bolt grinned as he watched Scott accuse Randal of corrupting the girl. He couldn't help himself. His laughter boomed through the room, causing the other men to look at him with guilt.

"You're bitching because you," he pointed towards Randal. "You ruined her for enjoying sex with just one man instead of two. Is that right?" He sat down on the small end table and slapped his denim clad thigh. "What the fuck? I thought the entire idea was to find a woman for all of us. I still haven't spoken to her without people around, but this woman sounds like she might know what she's looking for, and if she does enjoy multiple sex partners, you need to go to your knees and thank her."

Scott was clearly confused. He looked as if he hadn't slept in a day or two, and his hair stood out away from his head as if he'd been pulling on it. Randal just sat down with a can of soda and kept quiet.

Bolt shook his head and sighed. He had too much to deal with already but seeing Scott like this brought out his protective instincts. He reached over and pulled Scott toward him.

Scott knelt but stayed upright until he was engulfed inside the comforting arms of Bolt. He laid his head on the red head's shoulder and took several calming breaths. His arms came up to hold Bolt's shoulders, and he raised his head to string kisses along his jawline and neck. His head reclaimed the broad shoulder while he spoke.

"I'm sorry to bring this confusing shit to the meeting. She wants me; I can tell, but every time I try to say something about the future, it doesn't matter if that mention of the future is tomorrow, she changes the subject and puts me off. I can't do anything right. For instance, I ordered a pizza; she got bitchy. That was my fault. All I was trying to do was to feed her, and somehow I was supposed to know that mushrooms make her puke her guts out."

Bolt narrowed his eyes. He didn't like anything about this girl at the moment, but he didn't want to force Scott into defending her from a careless word coming from him. He kept his hold on Scott and angled his head to see what Randal was doing.

Randal was still sitting in the same spot with his head resting on the over-stuffed back of the sofa. He was watching the two of them, and when he met Bolt's eyes, he nodded. Something had to be done, and action needed to be taken so they could come to some kind of understanding with Lucy Posey. He'd never seen the overachieving, overly-confident, Scott, behave like this, and he didn't like it one bit.

He stood, pulling Scott's relaxed body up with him. "Tell you what; why don't you and Randal take a nap, or grab something to eat, and I'll be back in a few hours. I have some forms for the worker's comp claim, and maybe I can get to know her a little better." He raised his hand to Scott's face and lowered his head to kiss his lips. He took his time, and they were both breathing heavier and smiling when their lips separated. "I'll be back, so save me some of that." He patted Scott on the ass and nodded at Randal.

He and Randal had talked about what to do about Lucy while Scott was babysitting her at her house. He had admitted the attraction that she held for him, but beauty only went so far with him. A lot of women could make his cock hard, but if her character didn't match her looks, he would do his best to ween his friends off of her. He was going to demand some straight answers from the pretty blonde woman. Maybe he could figure out what to do about her.

If Scott hadn't been so sleep deprived and worn out, there would be no way that he'd have allowed Bolt to talk to Lucy on his own. Probably because Scott always said that Bolt was the mean looking one of them. Especially when he was pissed.

As he walked out of the door, he turned and saw Randal cradling Scott on his lap; the two men sharing an intimate kiss. He wanted to turn back and join them but knew that something had to be done about the woman. Randal's suggestion of a surrogate was beginning to look more appealing with each passing hour.

*****

Lucy could finally breathe a sigh of relief. Scott had left her alone for the first time all week, and she wanted to cry and laugh at the same time. He was temptation on two legs, and though this hormone thing seemed to intensify every emotion that she felt, she had resisted ripping his clothes from his body and having her way with him.

He had to be the most patient man in the northern hemisphere. She knew that she was being unfair in blaming him for her random bouts of depression. She blamed him for her nosy neighbors dropping by to "check on her." All those old gals wanted was to check out Scott's fantastic physique. Their concern for her wellbeing seemed to end at the doorway. Aside from a polite," Hello, dear," she was ignored by the ladies.

She had missed Pauline's funeral, but Anne had excused her once she saw the shape Lucy's face was in. Anne wasn't immune to Scott either. He was so polite to the ladies, even walking a few of them home if they'd stayed a "bit later than they wanted to." Lucy had no idea who raised him, but she had to give them credit for his impeccable manners.

The mention of his future plans, or their future plans was a roadblock for her. If she married a man, she would want him to love her as much as she planned to love him. After meeting Scott's friends, her fantasy laced dreams haunted her during the days that Scott stayed to keep her company. He put up with her bitchiness and had been nothing but kind and loving in return. She didn't want to lose him or that offering of love that she saw in his eyes.

The truth was that she was confused about the way she felt about his friends. A woman in love with one man could acknowledge that his friends were handsome, but she didn't lust after them to the point of waking in the middle of the night from dreaming of being penetrated and touched by three different men all at the same time.

She thought that she'd come up with the perfect retort when he offered to marry her. When he added, "I think we can make a good marriage if we both work at it and want to make it happen." She'd decided to give him an excuse that was partially true. She didn't want to outright tell him a lie, but telling him that she'd developed a liking for having sex with two men should have stopped his plans for the future.

"I'm sorry, but after that night with the two of you, my fantasy came to life then. It was better than I ever dreamed. My heart pounded, I could swear I felt the blood rushing through my veins." She had kept eye contact with him the entire time she spoke. "I won't marry someone knowing that I would probably have a fling like that night again. I'm not a liar, and I won't start lying about something that important."

He had tried to talk to her several times after that, but she refused to listen. As nice and sweet as he was, he might agree to any arrangement, only to regret it later. No, she wouldn't lie to him exactly. She knew that he would be enough for any woman, she would not need more than him. The fantasy was a real thing. How many women dreamed of having two men, sometimes more if she was feeling needy and greedy at the time, to service her every need. She might have been raised in a strict home, but she wasn't inexperienced about sex.

Alan hadn't been the only lover she'd had. Her high school prom date was a horny eighteen-year-old with a pick-up truck and a pint of sloe gin. That had been the one time in her life that she was thankful that her grandparents were deaf as posts. She'd sung her way up the driveway, and giggled her way to her bed, passing out with no further noise. Her grandmother had noticed the smell of alcohol and had shaken her head every time she saw her for the next week.

Lucy took an afterschool job at the diner two blocks from the school so she could earn enough money to buy one of the neighbor's ancient cars. It was older than she was, but the former owners kept it in tip top condition. It was the car that her grandfather wrecked and died in. He wasn't even supposed to be driving anymore. The doctor wrote to the state and reported his hearing loss and also reported the increasing case of dementia that had been observed at Gramp's last doctor's appointment. He hadn't heard the train whistle, and the crossing didn't have gates.

He was barely in the ground before her grandmother died in her sleep. She believed that Grans had died of a broken heart. She was in excellent shape for an eighty-five-year-old woman. To go to sleep and not wake up was considered a blessing by the people that helped raise the young Lucy when her parents dropped her off for a weekend, and never came back to retrieve her. The neighborhood occupants had been her family from day one.

Lucy had never been so totally alone in her life as she was the day after Grans funeral. The house was silent; no yelling, no music. Just the sound of her sobs as she grieved for the only two people who'd loved her, and that she loved in return.

She shook her head and opened the door to go out to her car. She needed to get back into her routine as soon as possible. Her face was still black and blue. Although to be honest, it was more yellow and green. Her hair would cover the stitches as long as she kept the length in a low ponytail. Wondering if she should cut the waist length braid occupied her thoughts as she opened the car door.

Bolt watched her walk towards her sedan. Once she opened the car door, he knew that he needed to intercept her before he was left at the curb while she drove away. She certainly was concentrating on her task. She never looked away from the vehicle in her path. That was a dangerous habit that some people had. They were so caught up in their thoughts that they were startled like he'd just done to her by shutting the door.

Those eyes of hers were really spectacular. Watching them widen in surprise was worth the run from the curb to her driveway. They were now sliding away from his face, and he didn't like it. He wanted her to be focused on him.

A masculine hand pushed the door closed, and she squeaked. She turned her head and was surprised to see Bolt Cummings standing there. His handsome face was not smiling, and she couldn't tell what his eyes looked like due to the sunglasses perched on his nose.

She inhaled and tried to center herself. The man was handsome. He was single, and more importantly, he also made her nipples tighten every time she knew that he was near. Then, of course, there was that whole him being her boss thing. She plastered a smile on her face and asked him what she could do for him.

"I was just on my way to the grocery store. While I was out, I planned to stop at the shop and see if I needed to sign any paperwork or anything for the insurance company."

There. That was good, right? She hadn't even stuttered while talking to him. She had a bad habit of talking out loud to herself when she was stressed and had to actually bite her tongue to make certain she didn't fall into that habit while dealing with him.

"I'm lucky I caught you before you left then. I've got some paperwork for you to sign, and I think your paycheck from last week is in the envelope too." He smiled, nodded and walked back to his truck to retrieve the packet.

She was unlocking her front door by the time he was on the sidewalk, so he followed her into the house.

It was a nice little place with old fashioned furnishings. He looked into the doorway leading to the living room and had to smile. There was a large wooden console television prominently sitting in front of the largest window in the room.

He couldn't help but wonder how Scott liked watching the evening news on such an archaic piece of electronic equipment. Was there even a remote for the thing? The thought made him grin. Scott loved his gadgets, they all did, but Scott bought the newest thing when it became available. He turned back to set the manila envelope on the small table where Lucy was setting glasses of sweet tea across the table from each other.

By her arrangement of the drinks, he knew that she was attempting to keep everything business like. That worked for him, at least, for their initial conversation. He pulled out a chair and turned it around to straddle it. If he had to sit at a little table like this, he was going to be comfortable. The back of the chair would give him a place to put his hands if he got the urge to wring her neck, or bust her ass.

Scott was easy going and nice, but she put Scott through the ringer, and she would soon learn that Bolton Cummings was not a man to try that shit with. No matter how beautiful her eyes were. He emptied the envelope and pulled his pen from the inside pocket of his suit coat.

"Here we go. This first document explains your rights and our obligation to pay you for the time off of work due to your injuries, and, of course, the medical bills. There is a provision for paying mileage to the doctor's office and hospital for any testing or procedures. You can save your gas receipts or other transportation receipts, and turn them in for a full reimbursement." He passed the small booklet to her and sat waiting to see what she would do.

When she thumbed through the pages, he could tell that she was not reading the wording in the document. She saw her name printed under a line designated for her signature and picked up the pen to sign her name.

He knew that the documents were correct, but no one should blindly sign something like this. Damn. "I think you should read what you're signing. While we try to make sure everything is on the up and up, you might not agree with the provisions and want to have them changed before you sign."

Lucy knew that she was going to have to tell him of her reading disability. She could read simple words and a few words that she saw in day to day life. This legal stuff; there was no way that she would be able to read or understand most of it. She gave it one last effort to avoid telling her boss that she couldn't read above a fourth-grade level without help.

"I trust you; if you're half the man your father was, then everything written in this paperwork is fair and honest." She smiled and reached for the pen again. He took it out of her fingers and scowled.

"I think there's more than honesty going on here." He picked up her hand that was still lying on the table. His fingers went to her wrist, and he could feel her pulse jumping under the skin just under her thumb. Good, he smiled again and looked at her. "Now, tell me why you are hesitating to read what you were signing; all you looked for was a signature line. The line you have there, is the place where you sign if you want a redetermination of your claim. The line accepting what we are offering is on the last page of the document." He held her hand tighter as she tried to pull away from his grasp.

"Lucy, I'm not an enemy. I want nothing but to help you here. Well, truthfully, I want more than that; but for now, let's get the business dealings out of the way first. Now, why won't you bother to read the document?" He sat there waiting for her to speak, all the while he waited he was rubbing his thumb over the inside skin of her wrist.

His touch startled her at first, but once she stopped trying to yank her hand away, the soothing rub of his thumb felt strangely comforting. She knew that telling this man about her disability might cost her a job that she enjoyed. There didn't seem to be an alternative to confessing, so she blurted it out.

"I have a severe reading disability. It's something that I've learned to cope with over the years, and I can decipher most normal words. Legal papers I normally take to someone else to read over and tell me what they say. You brought them here, so I will have to either sign them now, or you can leave them for me to take to my friend." She looked at the cupboard that was directly over his shoulder and hoped that he didn't realize exactly how afraid she was that he'd fire her. "I hope me telling you this doesn't mean that you are planning to fire me from my job now."

She looked like she was about to burst into tears, and Bolt felt like he'd swatted a kitten or something equally evil. Dammit, seeing that look made him understand what Scott had been facing all week. Those eyes swimming in the liquid of her tears made his gut clench. He shook his head giving himself a few seconds to stop looking into those eyes.

Fuck. He'd been subjected to seeing her picture in a grainy photograph for weeks, and he had been interested. Each time he'd seen her face to face had upped his interest even more. He hadn't dared to show his interest in her at the hospital. She was hurt, and a man didn't evaluate a woman that he'd just met who was lying in the emergency ward with head trauma, for a sex partner. He'd noticed her assets, but he hadn't been dreaming of holding her in his arms until now.

She looked so miserable and brave at the same time that he wanted to cuddle her. That was another first for him. He always let females come to him if they wanted affection. This one made him want to go to her and pick her up and carry her to a comfortable spot just to hold her until her misery was gone.

The longer he kept silent, the more certain she was that he was going to find a reason to fire her. She'd taught herself how to read the blueprints and understand the numbers that she needed to use for her job so it wasn't like he could claim that she couldn't do the work. Him being management, he could think up all sorts of reasons to fire her, and she wouldn't be able to do a thing about it.

She'd learned ways to deal with her impairment over the years. So far, she hadn't come up against a problem that she couldn't find a way to overcome. When people talked about the latest best-selling book, she was delighted to be able to join in the discussion. The books that she "read" were audio books. That habit had made her life much easier when dealing with her peers. Listening to the books in the car made the drive go faster, and kept the story lines fresh in case she needed to reference a point.

"Look, my dyslexia has no effect on my job or performance for the company, so you have no grounds to get rid of me because of it. Just let me sign the papers so I can get my back pay, and I will be at my job on Monday morning, as usual."

She didn't know that her voice went higher with every word she spoke. It took him a second to figure out what she was afraid of. She thought that he would fire her for a reading disability? Why the idea hurt his feelings, he didn't know.

A lot of people looked at him and drew the wrong conclusions. He couldn't help looking more like a lumberjack dressed for his own funeral, while at work. It didn't matter how expensive the suit was or who the tailor that fitted him was, most people backed up a step when meeting him for the first time.

She didn't appear to be afraid of his physical appearance. She had stood and begun pacing the small room, babbling about the rights of disabled persons in the workplace. "You cannot fire me for anything pertaining to my work performance. I do everything required and more, so I will sue you if you try to get rid of me."

She finally came to a stop in front of the chair he was sitting on. He smiled. She wasn't scared of him, and that was great as far as he was concerned.

"Lucy, I have no plans to fire you from a job that you've held for how many years? No, whatever personal things happen between you and Scott or Randal, has nothing to do with your employment. I am faced with a problem, though."

He stood up, and she backed away two steps. "You don't realize what I mean do you? I can see the puzzlement in your eyes."

He decided to let her figure it out on her own. The urge to pull her into his embrace and kiss her was becoming too strong, and he needed to think about this. With so much happening in his life, was he ready to commit with the other two to a woman that he barely knew? She was certainly pretty enough, and her eyes made him wonder how they would look with the sheen of love or sexual excitement coloring the jeweled blue orbs.

"Let's go over these papers and you can either trust me or take them elsewhere before signing them. Once we're done with business, I'll take you out for dinner, and we can get to know each other better."

By the time they had gone through each sheet of paper and he had answered her questions to her satisfaction, Bolt held a new respect for Lucy's intelligence. The woman was smart. She calculated the percentage of her normal wages and even averaged out the overtime she'd clocked in the past months. He didn't bother to check her calculations, he took her at her word and wrote the corrections down before they each initialed the page.

He grinned and told her to grab her purse. "I promised you dinner, and I'm starving. Let's go." He walked over to the door to wait for her.

Lucy wasn't sure that she wanted to continue to spend time with Bolt. The man was sexy, and she couldn't stop herself from staring at his lips when he spoke. She wanted to taste him, and that was a problem for her peace of mind.

What in the hell is wrong with you? First, you act like some porn star and take on two men at once; now you want to try their buddy out for size?

Bolt could tell that she was about to try to make excuses, and he wasn't about to let her get away with that. "Come on, I want a steak, and Shorty's has the best t-bone that you've ever tasted. The meat melts in your mouth."

He snagged her arm and pulled her out the door so fast that she squeaked when she missed the single step down. His hold was strong enough that she didn't fall down, but she still gave him a dirty look. His laughter was the only reaction that her look elicited. When he opened the door to the tall profiled truck, she turned to walk to her own vehicle and started to tell him that she would follow in her car. He actually picked her up and set her on the seat of the truck, and she was impressed. No one had picked her up since she was a small child.

She sat still, lost in her thoughts as Bolt got into the driver's side and started the engine.

"Why not? Two months ago, you were talked into going out with friends to celebrate your birthday. You end up having unbelievable sex with not one man, oh no, you had to double the pleasure with two of them. Now you're attracted to another man." She shook her head and raised her hands to her face, and then let them fall back to her sides. "What's next; five men? This is ridiculous. You're not a nympho for chrissakes."

Bolt was doing his best to keep his laughter silent. Both Scott and Randal had told him that Lucy talked to herself a lot, but this was his first experience with her habit. He slid a quick glance her way, and was amused to see that she was still talking to herself, but the words that her lips were forming had no sound.

It was a quick drive to Shorty's, and if she'd continued to berate herself out loud, Bolt knew that he would have turned around and taken her to the condo that the three men shared. They would all need to have a get together to discuss the possible relationship between them soon. Looking at her pouty lips made him look forward to the discussion. His body was fully interested in furthering their relationship, but his brain was holding out for more assurance that she was the women needed to complete their family.

He lifted her from the seat of his truck and enjoyed holding her tighter than necessary for an extra moment, before setting her on her own feet. He didn't resist the temptation to keep his arm around her shoulders as they walked into the steakhouse.

Lucy felt the soft kiss on the top of her head and wondered if Bolt was treating her like a child or if kissing her lightly on the head was his idea of a caress. She liked it, regardless of his motives. Several women tried not to be obvious or get caught looking at the big man in the expensive suit, with a killer smile, and it gave her reason to boldly look back at the women with a smug smile.

Being with Bolt during a meal was hilarious. She had to concentrate and make sure that he'd told her the punchline to his jokes before she swallowed her drink or the food in her mouth. He was entertaining her with stories of his and Scott and Randal's younger years.

"Randal's grandfather was a cool old dude; he knew that we used to hide out in the gardener's shed and drink whatever alcohol we'd swiped from our homes. I actually believe that he left a quart of moonshine out where we could get a hold of it. I don't ever remember being that sick in my life before, since we drank that stuff."

He grinned and shrugged at her smile. "What can I say, we were precocious. Scott's older brothers used to buy beer for us sometimes, but usually only if we blackmailed them. His mother is one of those women that make you want to cut your own tongue out so you won't say something to get one of her disappointed looks. Talk about guilt, if she gave you the guilt look, you felt it. The thing is that his brother's never figured out that we weren't about to tell on them; they were bigger and meaner than we were."

"So tell me about you. I've been spilling my guts out here, and you haven't been taking the stories of my misspent youth seriously. Laughing at my misery from the moonshine hangover isn't really a sympathetic response." He bit into a piece of the bloody looking steak and waved his fork her way.

Lucy had to swallow back the stuff threatening to come up from the sight of that bloody cow that was being devoured across the table from her. She looked at her own plate of grilled trout and concentrated on the beautiful flaky texture of the delicious fish.

"Well, I don't know what to say. I don't have friends like yours, but it sounds like you had a wonderful childhood. I envy you. As you know, my grandparents raised me." She shrugged as if her next revelation didn't still sting even after all of the past years. "My parents didn't figure out that they shouldn't be parents until I was born and they found out that a crying baby isn't as much fun as they thought I would be. They dropped me off at my grandparent's house for the weekend and never came back to get me."

She took a bite of the fish and moaned as she chewed and swallowed the delicacy. She wasted no time finishing the meal in front of her. There was nothing on the plate that she didn't like, and by the time she wiped her fingers on the napkin, the only thing left was a small pile of bones. She looked up to see Bolt looking back at her with a small smile on his face.

"What; is there a piece of asparagus in my teeth?"

He shook his head no, but the smile remained.

"Sure, don't tell me that I dribbled food on my shirt or whatever it is about me that is amusing you."

He laughed at that, and she licked her lips wishing it was his lips she was licking. The man was handsome, and she loved his sense of humor. The affection that he spoke of his friends with really did make her a little jealous.

"I'm not laughing at you, Lucy; I'm actually thinking up excuses to extend our time together. I enjoy being with you, you can appreciate my humor, and trust me when I say, that not many people think I'm funny." He tilted his head sideways and blinked his eyes at her and pursed his lips.

The laughter at his silliness bubbled out of her, and she couldn't help the shout of laughter that she let loose.

Once she caught her breath and wiped the tears from her eyes, she picked up her fork and pretended to stab herself in the chest. "I swear I haven't laughed so hard in as long as I can remember." She set the fork down and reached to squeeze his hand. "Thank you for such a delicious dinner, and thank you for being such an entertaining dinner companion."

The waitress stepped over with her order pad and asked if they wanted dessert. Lucy declined, but Bolt ordered a slice of blueberry pie.

"I can't help it; I'm a sucker for pie. I love the stuff." He wasn't smiling when he asked her to be level with him.

"I know that you had a rough time of it as you grew up, but how can I get to know you if you don't share something of yourself? Good or bad, you know that I won't ridicule you. I admire you, if the truth needs to be said. Hell, you've grown up and learned coping methods by yourself until you met that friend of yours. That is quite an accomplishment you know."

She knew that he wouldn't want to feel pity for her, but sometimes you had to decide to jump a hurdle in order to grow.

"By the time they diagnosed me with Dyslexia, I was being pushed through my grades and classes. I was too old to be in certain grades, so my name slipped through the cracks when it came time to teach me something. If it wasn't for one of the retired teacher's in the neighborhood, I would never have graduated from high school. There's a law in this state that helps people like me, especially kids with learning disabilities. I was finally diagnosed, so they had to provide me with someone to read the questions when we had quizzes or tests. It was embarrassing to have to go to the counselor's office to take them, but I started to pass my classes."

She took a drink from her glass of wine and shook her head. "There is a program for your computer that is called "read me" or something like that. It has been years since I've tried to get books loaded on the program, so I'm sure they've come up with something newer, but to me, it was a miracle. I'm not stupid or too dumb to learn; I just see things differently than other people.

"My friend taught me not to get so frustrated when I don't grasp something as quickly as most people do. I can laugh now, but at the time, it caused me a lot of stress."

He was nodding his head and still had that small smile on his lips. She looked around the room for inspiration for another subject to talk about. Seeing an older couple readying to leave the dining area gave her what she needed, and she launched into a funny story about her neighbors. When she told him about Scott being confronted the first day he'd been at her home by Miss Eloise, he was snorting and red in the face as he laughed.

Lucy couldn't resist leaning forward as if letting him in on a secret. "Miss Eloise has a crush on Scott. Every night when she's out for her walk, she stops to have a cozy little chat with him. Last night that hussy was wearing lipstick when she came to the door. He's been roped into escorting her home twice because it was too dark for a lady to be out roaming the streets by herself." She nodded her head to let Bolt know that he could let go of the air that he appeared to be holding in while she talked about the sweet lady that gazed at Scott with dreamy eyes.

Heads turned their way when he laughed. He was still chuckling as they left the building. He almost tossed her up into the seat of the truck, before going around and getting into the driver's seat and shook his head.

"I swear I haven't laughed so hard in years. I can actually see Scott treating the woman the same as he'd treat his own mother. Does he realize that Lady Eloise has a thing for his tender young body?"

His question sparked a debate on whether Scott wore blinders when it came to women, or if he humored them rather than allow any situation to become uncomfortable.

"As a woman who's seen him with and without clothes, I have to say the man does have that certain something that most women would find sexy as hell. I mean, look at his smile. When I saw him dancing almost nude and crawling towards me, trust me when I tell you that there was no way for me to refuse his hand reaching out to take mine."

Talking about Scott's sex appeal to Bolt, seemed a little crazy. After all, Bolt held a great deal of sex appeal too. But he wasn't nude and crawling on all fours towards her at the time either. She smiled and shrugged. Where Scott was a sleek, sexy animal, Bolt would be a powerful, dangerous creature drawing a woman into his aura of strength. She didn't want to think about Randal Murphy and his muscles.

Bolt heard her mumble something that sounded like, "Lord, those muscles. No, you don't want to think about those, or you'll probably climb him like a tree the next time you see him." He smiled and checked the rearview mirrors in an effort to keep his mind on the traffic.

He was finding out that she was making it easy for him to begin developing more than a passing interest in her. He was attracted to her body, no question there; it was her personality and ethics had been his main stumbling block, and she was dismantling that without trying.

He drove the truck into the supermarket parking lot, and Lucy geared up for an argument. He got out of his side and came over to hers to help her down. When he waved towards the store and told her to, "Go get what you need. I have to make a call, and I seriously doubt that you want me to tag along while you compare prices or pinch melons or whatever you do."

He turned to walk back to his side of the vehicle, and she frowned but walked into the grocery store. Why argue about something so simple? She'd planned to go shopping earlier anyway, so at least she would have help carrying the sacks into the house. "That's right; there's almost always an upside if you look for one."

She ignored the look that the stock boy sent her way when he realized that she was talking to herself.

Chapter 11

Lucy made it through the first week back on the job with a new appreciation for the sheer physical demands that was part of her work on any given day. Nicky had been learning the inspection part of the job before the attack. While she was off of work, Nicky had tried to keep up, but there was still a few thousand parts that needed to be inspected and packed in boxes to ship to the buyers.

The first two days, Loris was acting out of character by sending Nicky and Lauren to help get the mess taken care of, and on the third day, he came over to her table and looked at the two shelves that were left and told her that she was on her own now.

"You can handle the rest. I need to keep an eye on Nicky when she uses the soldering iron. She keeps melting holes in the boards. Sometimes I think she does it on purpose just to piss me off." He shook his head and frowned as Nicky wandered to her work station and set down a bottle of cola. That was a big no-no, and the little woman knew it.

Lucy knew why Nicky had begun a campaign of screwing up whenever Loris was looking her way. They'd talked while working together, and Nicky let her in on the secret that she and Loris were seeing each other outside of the workplace. "He has a habit of spanking my naughty butt." She'd giggled and grinned as she watched their boss walk over to talk to one of the maintenance men.

"He's one of those alpha-y, dominant men, and I have to say, I like it." She elbowed Lucy in the side and added, "He's also got the biggest cock I've ever ridden; I like that too."

The women had laughed at the time, but Lucy had a hard time looking Loris in the eyes now. Her eyes kept zeroing in on the man's zipper before she could stop herself from looking there.

She blamed the loss of her reservations on the three men that were rapidly pulling her into their circle. Thinking of the plans they'd made for the evening made her groan. She pulled into her driveway and was surprised that there was no one already there in the house waiting for her to get home. The guys had been taking turns staying overnight at her place since her dinner with Bolt.

Randal had been at the house when they'd stopped the big truck in front of her place. He had carried in groceries and had spoken to Bolt outside while she put the food away. From that night on, they had been a neighborhood attraction for the elders. Miss Eloise still had a crush on Scott, and she whispered to Lucy that she could appreciate a handsome man, even at her advanced age.

Since no one was waiting for her, she decided to take a nice long bath and steam some of the muscle aches away. Last night

Scott had taken her to the lake. His arms had come around her while they stood on the rocky shore and watched the storm come inland over the western horizon of the churning water. It was exciting to watch the lightning striking the water so far from where they stood. The wind and dark clouds rolled over and around the last two people out in the open. They stood in the light rain, and it wasn't until the lightning came closer to shore that they ran for the car. They'd laughed as they ran, and within seconds of the doors closing behind them, the heavens opened up and dumped heavy rain over the world outside of the confines of the small vehicle.

Not that they'd paid much attention to the rain. Scott had hit a switch, and her seat laid back into a reclining position, then his lips were kissing her laughing mouth within seconds of her entering the car. His hands were busy plumping her breasts and teasing her nipples while he kissed her.

Not that she had been lying there doing nothing to encourage his sensual assault. She'd traced his tongue with her own, and ran her short fingernails down his back as far as she could reach. She knew that she was playing with fire, but that didn't stop her from sliding her hands down the back of his shorts and filling her hands with the cheeks of his ass. She couldn't resist giving them a squeeze, and he nipped at her lips and laughed.

"You keep doing that, we're gonna' fog the windows up, and I'll be so deep inside of you that we'll both pass out from the pleasure."

She squeezed again, and he groaned while he pinched her nipple harder. She raised her chest, pushing up towards him to let him know that she liked what he was doing.

"If that was a threat, it wasn't a very effective one. I liked it when you were in deep before. What makes you think I would be worried about a repeat performance?"

She pulled her hands out of his pants slowly and held his jaw up so she could see his face when she made her confession to him. "I actually loved having you inside of me. I don't know what caused me to act like that, that night, but I still don't regret it. The only thing that bothers me is that I came away pregnant and had no idea that I might want a child until I lost the baby. I don't want to do that again. It hurts too much. I was careless and paid the price for being irresponsible."

It was the first time she'd mentioned the pregnancy; the first time that he would talk about his feelings of loss too. He rolled off of her and raised her seat back into the upright position. Leaning over, he gave her a tender kiss, pulled the seat belt around her and snapped it into place before starting the car and driving them home.

All he said as they left the beach was, "Let's talk about this at your place."

*****

It was still raining hard when they ran from the car into the house, and Scott peeled his shirt off at the door while he kicked off his shoes. Lucy flipped her sandals off and ran to the linen closet to grab towels for the two of them. Seeing him standing by the door without his shirt, and watching as he started to peel the soaked shorts down his sexy ass, made her pause for a minute.

"Oh for chrissakes, look at that. I swear Nicky is right."

The sound of her voice brought his head up to look at her standing just in the doorway of the small entry. She was clutching towels in her arms and staring at him while licking her lips. He smiled when he deciphered her low-spoken words.

"Really, what was Nicky right about?" He walked over to where she stood, pulled one of the towels from her arms, and began to wrap it around her shoulders.

He leaned in and snuck a kiss on her lips, before wrapping a towel around his waist after he gave her another quick look at his naked body. He smiled as he worked the t-shirt from her body, and the towel she was wearing dropped between them.

"I'm sorry, let's just get out of these wet clothes, and dry off before one of us catches a cold. Although I do think you have the hardest nipples that I've ever seen, and I really want to enjoy playing with them. From what I remember, I didn't get the chance to taste them before, so I'll make sure that I take care of that tonight."

She bent and picked up the fallen towel and wrapped it around her dripping hair. She swatted his busy fingers as they worked on the button of her shorts to help her out of the wet denim.

"I can do that myself; you've been more than helpful." She turned her head and began to turn to walk into the hallway to her bedroom, but he pulled her hand and led her to the sofa in the living room.

He shook his head back and forth with a frown on his handsome face. "I said we'd talk, and we're going to. I'm not some ass that is just out for sex, at least, not right this minute, so drop the damn shorts. You can cover up with the blanket thing."

It wasn't worth starting an argument over. She wasn't going to fight against something that she actually wanted, but felt shy about asking for. She glanced at him once she was seated on the cushions, and he plopped down on the middle section. She let him pull her knees up onto his lap, shivering when he ran his warm hands over her knees to pull them closer.

Scott tried to organize his thoughts before opening his mouth and sticking his foot inside. He prayed silently for the words to tell her how he felt about the baby that neither of them would ever get to hold. He owed her that.

"I promised to talk, so here we go." He looked up and shifted his body slightly sideways. This new position helped him see how she would react to his explanation. "That night, I was filling in for Aaron, he's one of the dancers, but his wife was sick, so I took his spot in the show. I don't strip and dance much anymore. When we first bought The Zoo, Randal and I both took our turns every weekend night on stage."

He heard her giggle and gave her a look. "Yeah, yeah. I know that he doesn't look like a dancer, but he's actually really good. The women got all clingy, and I swear that they would come just watching that overgrown ox do a stomach roll, or the crowd favorite, he would bring a woman on stage and allow her to ride on his back on the stage while he basically crawled like I did to you that night."

He laid his head back and yawned before starting to talk again. She was playing with the fingers of his hand that rested on her naked thigh.

"Anyway, long story shorter, Randal only dances when there is no one else to fill in, and Bolt, well he has rhythm, just not for dancing like we do. It's great exercise, but since none of us dance regularly anymore, we need to find a gym."

"That night, I saw you, and I was attracted to your hair. No, don't look so skeptical. Some men like eyes, some like to see a woman's tits or ass, I happen to like beautiful hair. Once you sat down and looked at me, I was done. I swear your eyes are the prettiest eyes I've ever looked into like that. I won't lie, I've known some beautiful women, I've had sex with a few of them too."

He picked up the hand that was toying with his fingers and kissed her knuckles. "I never, not once, had the reaction that I had to you that night. Looking into your eyes, I had to have you. I don't do that; I don't ever have sex with a patron in one of the bars. I won't even make a date with the women that come in."

He rubbed the fingers in his hand and pulled her onto his lap, by hooking his other arm around her waist and shifting them together. He urged her to lay her head on his shoulder as he continued.

"You don't have to believe me; you can ask Randal, Bolt, or anyone that works at the bar. I don't act recklessly like that. Yet, there I was, lying on that cold damned floor with the hardest cock I've ever had, and all for a woman that I had never met before. You don't know it, but I'm not sure I wouldn't have had you right there on that stage if Randal hadn't helped out with the lights."

His hand rubbed her back, and she sighed. His reaction to her closely mirrored hers to him. "I felt pretty much the same as you did. I don't do that kind of thing, not ever." She sat up to look him in the eyes. "I swear, the last thing on my mind was getting pregnant. I told myself that I needed to step out of my comfort zone and do something crazy. After all, it was my birthday; I should go a little wild, right?"

Scott gave her a nod and a small smile. "I had the condom; I barely remembered to roll it on, but after I had come, I noticed that the damn thing had broken. The thought of possibly getting you pregnant filtered through my mind, but it never stuck. I ran out to deal with a fight between some women in the bar because Randal was still busy with you, and by the time I came back, you were gone.

"I came back thinking that we could have another round of lovemaking, but you didn't even leave your number; you just vanished. I'm now sure of one thing; I couldn't make myself give up hope that we'd find you again. The last day, I'd been so discouraged over my failure to find even the smallest clue looking for you. On the same day that Randal texted me to come to the hospital, I had decided to stop looking. Fate decided that it was time to give me a push in the right direction."

He pulled her tightly to his chest again and held her in his arms. "I have never felt for another woman what I feel for you. I don't know if its love, but it damn sure feels like it is." He bent his head to nuzzle her jaw. "I want you, but I didn't bring anything with me for protection, so unless you have a box of condoms hiding somewhere, what I want isn't happening tonight. You need to know that you aren't alone in feeling the loss of the little one.

"Knowing that you were carrying my baby brought me to my knees. Losing it... that was hard for me to hear." They were silent for a few minutes, drawing strength from each other. He broke the quiet by saying," You must be pretty mad at me about the baby."

Lucy pulled herself upright again. "I am *not* mad at you. I was there too. Remember? It seems that there is plenty of blame to go around here. We both blame ourselves, but I talked to the doctor and two of the nurses. They all told me that the baby might not have grown and lived anyway. If the fetus had been set right, or whatever, I wouldn't have lost it. I can blame that woman; I can blame you. The truth is, I was the one that walked into the bar that night. I can only blame myself."

She stood up, forgetting that the towel stayed on the arm of the sofa, as she walked toward the kitchen wearing just a pair of panties and her white skin.

Scott followed close behind her and stopped her by taking her shoulders in his hands. He turned her and saw the tears streaming down her cheeks and the misery that she could no longer hide. She was holding back, but he wasn't going to let her.

"Dammit, you're not to blame for the miscarriage. You know that. I talked to the doctor too, you know. There was nothing you or anyone else could have done to prevent the loss of the baby. Nothing. I'm not going to let you take on blame for something that you didn't even know was possible."

She shook her head as he was speaking. "Nicky teased me about a 'bun in the oven' and I had symptoms. I tried to ignore the idea, but I knew something was wrong with me. When they told me I had lost my baby- our baby, I didn't believe it; I couldn't believe it. If I believed it, that meant that I'd never told my baby I loved it." She completely broke down after the last two words.

Scott picked her up, carrying her into her bedroom and sitting on the bed with her still cuddled close. Her heartbreak made his eyes tear up. He'd spent hours riding the bike to help deal with the idea of a child lost too soon. She hadn't had an outlet until now, and no matter how long or loud she needed to grieve, he would stay with her. She wasn't alone.

He spent the next hour holding her and rocking them both, trying to soothe the pain and guilt. Logically he knew that they had nothing to feel guilty over, but he was not about to start that subject up again tonight. That one would be better off talked out when the time was right.

Chapter 12

She was going on an outing with one of the three men in her life. There was no way to mistake that the men seemed to be courting her. How they figured that would work, she had no idea, but they didn't shy away from hugging her or kissing her deeply in front of each other. Fantasizing about having sex with two men at a time was easy. Each time she attempted to add a third man to her dreams, she got messed up in the "who's hands went where." She was happy. She grinned at odd times during the days following the heart to heart that she had with Scott.

Randal showed up the next morning, and they went out for lunch, but when he told her to dress for a hike in the woods, she thought he was joking.

"I've never been in the woods in my life. Why would anyone want to go looking for poison ivy and pricker bushes?"

He laughed at her. "You need to expand your little world. I know what poison ivy looks like, and I have bug spray so you won't have to worry about being bitten. Although we can still spend a while when we get home checking each other for ticks. They are some nasty little bastards."

He sprayed her down with some stinky stuff, and they drove to the state park to explore the trees and wildlife. The sight of two deer gave her quite a thrill. When Randal pulled her away from a plant, she thought it was the dreadful ivy, but he shook his head and used a stick to pull the leaves back to expose a brown snake that had slithered under the plant.

"He's just a blow snake, but you wouldn't know that, and if you saw him and got scared, you might scream and scare the other wildlife away."

By the time that they'd returned to the truck, Lucy was ready to collapse.

"I thought I was in shape and could handle just about any kind of physical activity, but this is tougher than I imagined." She guzzled the bottle of water and had to fight back nausea from swallowing the icy cold liquid too fast.

Randal patted her back and murmured sympathetic noises while she stood with her hands on her knees doing her best not to be sick in front of him. "I should have warned you about that. Small sips work better than drinking the whole bottle like that. I feel like an ass. I never considered that you didn't keep fit with regular exercise, even hiking. How do you keep your figure?"

Lucy looked sideways at Randal and didn't think before she reacted to his half-hearted words of sympathy.

"I work like a dog in a factory. I stay in shape by staying on my feet all day lifting boxes of computer data boards, and basically filling in for whatever position needs someone to work it. I'm no prissy girly girl, but I don't need to waste my money working out at a gym, or wandering around in the woods by myself just to put more mileage on my tired feet."

Her nausea was forgotten, and she forced herself to stand as straight as possible for the walk back to the other side of the truck. The hike had taken more out of her than she wanted to admit.

Randal knew that she wasn't actually mad at him, but she did a good job of ignoring his attempts at small talk. He changed his plans for a night out with her on the town. He had to think fast, and remembered that his grandparents were in Georgia for the next few weeks. He still had a room in the main house, but the small guest house by the pool was the direction that he steered her towards.

"This is my family home, but my grandparents are gone for a while, and if we enter the main house, the security cameras will pick up every movement inside. I won't have time to run inside and punch in one of the three codes they use to shut it off before the Grands get a call that I'm here and brought a friend." He looked back at the house and shook his head at the small carousel that was a recent addition to the backyard. "If that happened, I would be getting a phone call within five minutes from one of them wanting to know who you were and when can they meet you."

He looked so serious the entire time that he spoke and watched the back door of the beautiful house. She had to grin and shake her head at him.

"Is this a case of sneaking a girl into the house when the parents are asleep? I missed that experience in high school. The closest I came to sneaking around parent's backs was driving to the river park and making out in the backseat of a boy's parent's car. The local cop almost always caught us and threatened to call our houses."

He turned a little pink around the neck but grinned back as she teased him. He opened the door to the cottage and stood back for her to enter first. Before he followed her inside, he waved at the security camera that was set in under the eaves of the three season room. If his grandparents saw the video, he wanted them to know that he was aware of their spying.

Lucy found a clean suit to change into after Randal pushed her towards the small bathroom. His, "Come on, let me make amends. I think I can promise to make your day more comfortable," was heartfelt enough that she gave in.

He was another man that had no problem wearing next to nothing while she tried to look like she wasn't ogling his body. The tight speedo that hugged his sculpted, muscular thighs and ass left little to the imagination. Her lips were getting chapped from constantly licking them while she fought the urge to knock him down and kiss and nibble her way over his sun-bronzed muscles.

His peace offering of a relaxing dip in the hot tub, followed by a nice long massage was a great way to restore her happiness for the day. However, the way his hands worked her muscles and his fingertips continually teased the inside of her thighs, and the sides of her breasts, defeated the promise of relaxation.

His lips kissed and licked their way across the span of her shoulders, and ringed the back of her neck with little sucking kisses while his fingertips teased the crease of her lycra covered ass.

She tried to roll over to lie on her back, but his hand spanned the small of her back to hold her in place. She shivered when she felt his warm breath waft near her ear.

"I owe you, and I always pay my debts. Just let me know if I'm not doing it right."

She felt him move and allowed his fingers to separate her legs wide enough for him to kneel between her knees. His hands ran up from the backs of her knees to the crease between thigh and cheek. Feeling his widespread fingers begin squeezing the pale globes made her moan.

The crotch of the suit was pulled to the side, so he had better access to the treasure of her welcoming slit. It was his turn to groan. "I know that you might not be impressed if you saw the view I'm looking at right now, but I swear it's the prettiest sight I've seen in forever."

She gasped and cried out when he slid two fingers inside of her pussy. She was so wet that there was only a feeling of being widened the deeper his fingers penetrated. When those fingers stopped going deeper and started to explore and search out the special places inside to play on and give her pleasure, she clenched her jaw on a scream of frustration.

Her hips couldn't remain still, and she raised and lowered them in an effort to establish a rhythm. She wanted his fingers to work on her body everywhere at once and ended up raising her hands to cup her breasts and pinch her nipples while his fingers spread her wider to add another finger for her pleasure.

His pinky was curled over her clit, and each time she raised her hips, it put pressure on the little muscle enhancing the mind-blowing pleasure that she was being treated to.

He leaned over her back and started whispering encouragement into her ear, "That's right, just let it happen. This is all for you today, and I want you to take whatever you want. I love the way your sweet pussy clamps down on my fingers. It makes me think of how tight you'll be once I get my cock buried in you so deep that you won't know where you end, and I begin."

She felt the way her pelvic muscles began to tighten in anticipation. Her hips raised and pumped back onto his hand while she groaned and cried out for relief. "Please, please," didn't cover what she wanted to say, but there was no way that she could articulate a sentence right now. Just as she started to tighten and clamp down on the fingers filling her, she came unglued from the feeling of Randal slowly pushing his thumb into her puckered asshole.

There was no way for her to remain still or to analyze why the pleasure took her breath until she lost her mind in ecstasy. Even as her legs collapsed and she lay on the massage table trembling, trying to catch her breath, he kept his hand in place. Her wet flesh was so sensitive that she cried out each time those long digits moved.

Randal smiled as he eased his fingers from her wet slit. She was so responsive to his touch that he almost regretted his decision to only give her a great orgasm. Scott told him how last night ended in tears and grief, and he felt the need to give her some happiness.

An orgasm wasn't lasting happiness, and it wouldn't change history, but for a few minutes it made her forget her pain, and that was why he'd given her this gift. He hadn't lied to her either. She had given him pleasure that night, and he had done nothing to make her pleasure peak. Now he had reciprocated, and his plans for the next round were forming in his mind.

If she had seen his smile when he lifted her from behind, bringing her to her knees, while he ran his hands down the front of her body, she might have asked him what he was thinking about. His lips kissed along her jawline and nipped at her earlobe.

"I want you, and I know that you can feel my cock begging to be inside of you. Does knowing how easy it is for you to make me hard give you a thrill? I'm not trying to hide it; I want to sink as deep inside of your tight pussy as I can get."

His lips continued to travel along her sensitive skin, and his hands kept shaping her breasts in his palms while teasing her nipples with those long fingers of his. Lucy couldn't stay still. She wanted him. The feeling of his thick cock so hard against the cheeks of her ass gave her a thrill. He was correct, knowing that she was the cause of his torment was a rush. She quickly found out that wiggling her ass over the stiff length of him was even more empowering. He groaned and bent his head down and his body away from her teasing.

"Woman, you need to stop doing that. I didn't bring condoms, and I want to come inside you too damn desperately to stop if you keep that up." He took a deep breath and let go of his hold on her, turning away and walking out the door fast.

She heard a splash and laughed. He'd jumped into the pool to cool off. She climbed down from the table and made her way into the small bathroom to change back into her own clothing. Randal's thoughtfulness and restraint impressed her, even if she wished that today's make out session had ended differently. He wasn't the only one that regretted not having condoms on hand. She imagined that he would feel amazing powering into her. He wasn't small, but she wasn't worried. She'd taken Scott's generous size; Randal's would work as well.

She tried to rationalize her feelings by blaming them for introducing her to the idea of multiple sexual partners but knew better. If she hadn't been interested before the experience, it had only been because she hadn't tried it.

Chapter 13

Telling them that she no longer wanted them to spend every night at her place had been hard. They had thought they would be sneaky by coming over one at a time and staying until she told them to leave.

The certainty that she would gladly have sex with any of the three men bothered her. The one thing that she did know was that she needed to take a few days away from them. For some reason, they had decided that she needed to have one of them in her guest room every night. Telling them that she was fine had done nothing to change their minds.

It was Friday and Nicky's birthday. The women were leaving work and would meet at Laurie's place at seven thirty. If the night went the way it normally did when the girls celebrated their birthdays, or pretty much any other good cause, they would eat when they got to the bar. After food would come drinking while watching sexy men strut their stuff for the enjoyment of the hundred or so women that flocked there when the male strippers were dancing.

Lucy broke the speed limit on the way home. She wanted to get into the house and leave before Bolt showed up tonight. She knew that she needed to lay the law down for the men, but if she was honest with herself, she enjoyed their company. Each man had a special attraction, but the strength of that attraction was exactly what worried her.

****

This shit was getting old. Bolt rubbed his face with his hand in an effort to gather his thoughts and calm down. He was tired of the courtship that Scott wanted them to give Lucy.

"I think we need to show her that we are great guys separately, that way she can appreciate our good qualities once we tell her that we want her to join our family. Knowing each of us and our personalities might help her decide that while we might be unconventional, we are worth loving."

Bolt had given in to the plan, but enough was enough. They'd been playing this "get to know me" stuff long enough. It was time to bring them all together and move forward. The only reason that he hadn't pressed her willing body for sex yet was legitimate. He was the owner of the company that she earned her paycheck from. Getting involved with her would be opening himself to a lawsuit. He found himself watching her from the office windows above the area where Lucy was in charge of the pod of workers.

If they got involved, she was going to have to quit working for F&P. She would resist that idea. After the hissy fit she threw when she thought he planned to fire her for a simple reading disability, he still couldn't come up with a way to make her see things his way.

Now he sat in her driveway, and she was not at home. He'd be damned if he allowed this to go on. He couldn't say for sure that he loved her, but she fascinated him. His body gave him its opinion each time she was within touching distance. The few times that they had hugged and kissed he had to back away before he pushed her into agreeing to have sex with him.

He could do it. From the enthusiastic responses that she'd given with each contact between them, he was confident in his ability to charm her. He found that he didn't want the need for physical lovemaking to be simply give and take. He wanted their encounter to be give and give to each other.

Tonight he would allow her the space that she had been requesting since they'd met in the hospital. Perhaps he would insist that the other guys give her breathing room too.

They could make a date to get everyone together and lay their hearts and cards on the table. Tomorrow was Saturday. He had the perfect excuse to invite her to accompany them. He was looking at homes. That way she could have some input if he found a home that would fit the bill in size and amenities.

Once he entered the apartment, he knew that something was wrong. He stalked through the rooms until he opened the bathroom door and found Randal with a bloody towel held to his head. Randal was laid out on the floor between the shower and the stool with his head lying on the lid of the commode. There were blood splotches on the porcelain, and Bolt had to swallow back the bile from his empty stomach that threatened to distract him from his friend. His phone was in his hand before he realized that he was calling for help.

He had to keep it together, but the only thing he could think of was that he couldn't lose another loved one. He held onto Randal's naked shoulders as he sent a text to Scott's cell phone. The tears swimming in his vision pissed him off. His father had always told him that men weren't supposed to cry, but fuck it. His father had cried when his wife was lying in that hospital bed, and love had a way of breaking down a man's resolve.

He crouched next to the tub and tried to raise Randal's hulking body from where it was wedged. As strong as he was, he couldn't budge the big man, so he sat on the floor waiting for the ambulance. He pulled Randal sideways, continuing to hold the blood-soaked towel in place.

"Come on man; you need to stay with me here. It's a good thing that Lucy skipped out on me tonight, or I wouldn't have been home in time to call for help. Damn you, don't die on me." He kissed the top of Randal's head. "We'll get you all fixed up, and then I plan on laughing my ass off at you for slipping on the soap."

He heard the doorbell and yelled as loud as he could to tell them to hurry up. He looked towards the doorway and saw an officer checking out the room before walking towards where they sat on the floor.

The medics were crowding the room within minutes, so Bolt was pushed from the small space while the paramedics worked on Randal and loaded him onto the backboard. It took him and the cop to help the medics carry Randal's body into the living room where they had a gurney waiting.

One of the medics was a pretty redhead with a beautiful smile, and she was fussing over Randal's body that was now covered with a pristine white sheet. Bolt cleared his throat to get her attention, but she was too busy fussing to pay attention. Her partner was an older man with a gold tooth that flashed as he smiled. He shook his head and grinned at Bolt.

"Your friend will be fine. Head wounds bleed like crazy, but he looks like he's in good shape, so he won't miss a pint or two of the red stuff."

They loaded Randal into the ambulance, and Bolt almost ran over the cop that was still standing around waiting to get a statement. He went through the events since he got home, doing his best not to get mad at the man that was only doing his job.

As soon as the officer left, Bolt locked the door behind him and walked into the bathroom to clean Randal's blood off of his body. He didn't normally clean the bathroom, that is what he employed the cleaning crew for, but there was no way he would leave Randal's blood spattered and drying all over the room. He found bleach and a bucket under the kitchen sink, and ruined his suit pants when he poured the bleach into the water in the bucket, but it was too late to worry about damaging his clothes anyway.

Once the job was complete, he stripped and got into the shower. He couldn't go to the hospital with bloody clothing and splattered bleach spots. The smell of blood and bleach seemed to be stuck in his sinuses, but standing with the water running over his head served to wake him up and erase the scents.

The emotions from the past few weeks were taking their toll on his normally invincible personality. Yet within such a short space of time, he had cried like a baby over his parent's deaths, and the feelings for Randal were choking him now. He didn't know what he needed to help him deal with this new side of himself. Whatever it was, he hoped he found it soon.

All the way to the hospital, he prayed for guidance. He wasn't much for religion, but his mother swore that God will send the answers to a person that asks for them. He was finding out that the notion comforted him as he spoke aloud in the confines of the truck's cab. Some people would have condemned his lifestyle and told him that bad things happen as a punishment. That was the main reason that

he'd refused to attend the church that he had been baptized in as a baby with his parents.

Today his talk with an entity that he only half believed in soothed his worry. He decided then and there that he would spend more time like this. After all, it made him feel better, and his sanity might depend on it if things continued to be as unsettled as they had been lately.

He wondered what was going on with Scott. He hadn't answered the text, and that was not like him. He would call when he found out how Randal was doing. As far as Bolt knew, Scott was spending the evening with his family. His mother talked him into showing up for dinner and to discuss some family business that she'd refused to talk about on the telephone.

Bolt had been to the Henderson house several times. The family was a riot, and there was always some drama happening. Scott did his best to help his siblings, but his efforts were rarely appreciated. He wasn't the oldest of the siblings, but he was the one everyone went to when they needed help.

By the time Bolt was allowed to see Randal, he was in a bad temper. Scott hadn't called or contacted him. Mrs. Henderson told him that Scott had left the house two hours ago, but she had no idea where he'd gone. She told him, "He got a phone call and took off out of here like a scalded dog." Her tone held anger, and that got factored into the mystery. Mrs. Henderson was never angry.

Bolt couldn't help but think Scott's disappearance had something to do with Lucy not showing up tonight. She wasn't answering her phone either.

Randal was in no shape to worry about the two absent people. Bolt didn't mention their disappearance. He hugged Randal and quietly told him that he would be back in the morning. "Don't act the martyr man, if you need me, call."

Randal had squeezed Bolts fingers before he drifted back to sleep.

Chapter 14

Scott was in the middle of his sister, her husband and his mother all trying to explain to him why he needed to loan his sister's husband enough money to start his own business. Everything was going well until Scott began asking questions.

"Let me make sure that I heard what you want me to loan you money for. You want a hundred thousand to start a car detailing shop and automatic car wash?" He looked at Darnel and received a grinning head nod.

"Okay, and you need start up money so you will be able to pay five employees, and your household expenses until the business gets going and paying for itself?" Another grinning nod. "You think the cash to start up and keep your family fed for at least six months to a year will be right around double the initial hundred grand?"

Darnell either didn't see the look of pity that Scott shot towards his sister and mother, or he was delusional. "I'm going to tell you what I think. You come to me through my mother, thinking she will sway me towards investing in a business that is failed before it starts. You have no business plan; you have nothing to invest on your end. You want me to basically hand you almost a quarter of a million dollars so you can sit on your ass and use my money to pay other people to work. You've been drawing disability for years now, and I would bet that there is a reason for this scheme of yours."

The guilty look that his sister shot towards her husband told Scott all that he needed to know. "I bet that you've been kicked off disability, and now you're looking for someone else to give you a free ride. Since I already bought the trailer that you live in so my sister and nephews don't have to live under a fucking bridge, why not try to get more from me." It wasn't a question.

Scott balanced himself because it looked like Darnel was going to make the mistake of taking a swing at him. His cell phone began to ring at the same time his sister grabbed her husband's arm to stop him from trying to gain revenge for Scott's refusal to play the patsy.

The call was from The Zoo. They never called him unless there was something that the managers couldn't handle. He turned his back to the people in the room and began walking away. First the shit with Darnel, and now Aaron was calling to tell him that his blonde and her friends were back in the bar, and the women were all drinking heavily.

"Blast it. Okay, keep an eye on Lucy and what's-her-face. I'll be there in about an hour. I'll have to stop off and swap the bike for the car since she's drinking. I don't know if she likes to ride or even if she's ever been on a bike, but I'm not taking any chances."

His mother stepped closer to him when he turned back to tell her that he was leaving. He hated to see the worry for his sister on the older woman's face. She was the glue that held the family together, he didn't want her to worry, but he was not about to hand over that kind of money to a deadbeat either.

"Mom, I love you, and you know I would do anything I can to help the family." He held out his hand to point in the direction of the back deck where Darnell was smoking a cigarette and yelling at Linda.

"If she doesn't want to change her life, that's up to her. I'm not financing that bum so he can play the big shot while my sister does the work. He hasn't changed from when he was in high school. Just another lazy bum that got lucky and married a woman willing to work hard enough to keep him in beer and smokes."

He put his arms around his sweet mother and hugged her tight. She was losing weight again, and he knew that she needed to get away from all of the drama shit that someone, no matter which someone it was, would start.

He bent his head over hers and quietly asked her to slow down a little. He drew back and crouched a little to look at her beautiful face. "You can't help someone who isn't willing to help themselves; isn't that what you used to tell me all of the time? I won't mortgage my future children's lives to make Darnell a temporary big shot. Please stop letting them hurt your heart."

He let her go and kissed her on the cheek before heading to the door.

The ragged old tom cat sitting on the seat of his bike hissed at him when he reached to pick him up to move him. He swatted the seat behind where the cat sat, and it worked to move the feline. He smiled, after all, the more things stayed the same, the more comfort he got from little stuff like the mangy assed cat spitting at him.

He started the bike and rode away. He was going to have to do something to take the stress off of his mom's shoulders. At least he could give her a respite. The vacation cruise that he, Bolt and Randal had planned to give her for her birthday should help. She could take her friend Wendy with her, and he hoped that being away from home for two weeks would rejuvenate her. She had lost the sparkle in her eyes, and if Darnel was the cause of her unease, Darnel would be one sorry bastard.

He pulled into the driveway and put the bike inside the garage before running inside to get his car keys.

The smell of bleach was so strong that it burned his eyes when he passed by the bathroom. He didn't see the source but assumed that the cleaning people had just left.

He grabbed his keys and ran out to the car. His mind was working overtime as usual. He was wondering why Randal's truck was in the garage, but Randal wasn't home. He was also concerned that the door had been left

unlocked. The issue with his brother-in-law
was filed in the back of his mind. He knew that
Darnell wouldn't give up so easy.

He wondered what the women were
celebrating tonight at The Zoo. Lucy confided
in him that they always celebrated things like
birthdays, bachelorette parties, and even once
a retirement party for one of her neighbors that
wanted to see male strippers. He had laughed
when she'd described the way her elderly
friend had bragged to the ladies at the Senior
Center about her trip to the bar.

Walking into the bar was fun. Two ladies
were talking and hanging onto each other, and
he had to ask them twice to excuse him for
trying to walk inside further than the doorstep.
He got such a hostile look from the one with
the goth make-up that he just shouldered his
way around the women. Aaron saw him
walking through and waved him over to the
bar.

"Hey, man, your girl has been sitting in the
same place since she got here. The only thing
she got up for was to use the ladies room. Her
friends, on the other hand, have been pretty
loud. That brunette got up on stage with Jack,
and she pulled his thong off. I had to haul her
off of the stage, but she was right back up
there when Billy was dancing. The other girl;
that slender bleach blonde? Baby's got a
mouth on her. She followed two of the waiters
into the back room, and one of them came out

fast; the other one was Mickey, he eventually came out with a smile on his face.

"The thing is, I looked for your girl right after I talked to you, and she was gone. I don't have time to go out and look for her, but her friends are saying that she's a big girl and can fend for herself. They aren't concerned."

Scott checked his cell phone and cursed. The battery was dead. He nodded to Aaron, who was back slinging liquor bottles while the ladies standing around the bar cheered him on. The place was certainly rocking tonight.

He wove his way through the myriad of perfumed females, to reach the office. He could plug in the cell phone and use the landline to call Bolt and Randal. Hopefully, one of them either had her with him, or they knew where she took off to.

He walked into the room and stopped in his tracks. Lucy was stretched out on the couch, sound asleep. Her arm cradled her head, and he had to smile when he heard a small snort coming from her mouth as she slept. Her shoes were next to the table. Scott grinned as he rounded the desk to plug his phone into the charger cord.

The screen lit up as soon as the battery had enough juice, and the thing kept dinging; letting him know that he had several messages. He scrolled through the texts and felt his heart drop. Bolt's voice went from near panic, to very worried as Scott listened to the voice messages. He quickly texted back to tell him about his dead cell battery.

He had to stay at the desk to keep the connection for the phone and cursed himself for not plugging the damn thing in last night. Randal was hurt, and Bolt was alone to deal with the situation. Knowing him, Scott could only imagine the panic that Bolt had felt finding Randal bleeding and out cold. Thankfully, Bolt had found him in time to get help.

He looked towards the couch, hesitating to call Bolt for fear of disturbing her nap, but screw it. Randal and Bolt were more important than a few minutes of sleep. He used the landline that was sitting on the desk.

"Hey, man, I'm so sorry about Randal. What happened?" He was so happy to hear Bolt's voice answering on the first ring that he wasted no time asking questions.

Bolt's voice was raised, but all Scott heard was concern and worry in his tone. The initial rundown of his list of complaints made Scott smile. If he could make a mental list like that, then he was calming down from the initial knee-jerk panic of nothing going right in Bolt's schedule for the night.

"You didn't answer your cell, Randal was bleeding like crazy, and to top it all off, Lucy is nowhere to be found. That turned out all right, I guess. If she had been home, I wouldn't have gone back to the apartment and found Randal. What the fuck, man? I can't deal with this shit. All I thought of when I found him lying there bleeding all over the place," he took a deep breath, "All I could think of was that I can't lose anyone else that I love."

Bolt didn't say anything else until Scott told him, "I found Lucy. She's here at The Zoo. It looks like the ladies are celebrating something. Aaron called me to let me know that the women showed up earlier. I came to the bar and found no sign of Lucy. No one knew where she went, so I came into the office to charge up my phone, and found her sleeping on the sofa."

He nodded his head in agreement while Bolt laid down his demand that they, "Sit her down and lay it all on the line. We'll just have to hope that she'll be willing to open her mind and her heart to include all three of us."

Scott sympathized with his friend. After all, Bolt's life had gone from a secure, carefree life, to a life of forced responsibility. He said goodbye, then walked over to the couch, sitting on the arm closest to where Lucy's blonde hair covered her face. She rubbed her cheek on the finger that lightly teased the dimple that made him want to make her smile. He would do a lot to see that cute little indent in her silky skin. He sighed and reached further down to her shoulder to give her a little shake.

"Hey, kitten, we need to get moving." She rolled onto her back and without his quick reflexes, she would have rolled onto the floor. He was on his knees at the edge of the cushion where she ended up wedged between his stomach and the cushion edge. One of her legs hung down with her foot on the floor, and she looked around the room in confusion for a minute.

Scott couldn't resist and didn't bother trying. He pulled her into his arms and laid a small kiss on her dimple. "I hope you're not in a hurry to get home; we have to stop at the apartment before I can take you back to your place."

Lucy looked at the handsome man and smiled, "I was too tired to keep up with Nicky and Lauren. I didn't think it would cause any trouble, or make anyone mad if I came in here for a quick nap. It's Nicky's birthday; I owe her a drink."

She hooked her arm around his neck and pulled herself up for a kiss. She snuggled into his embrace once both of his arms pulled her tightly against his body.

"I was dreaming about you; did you read my mind?" She continued to kiss his lips, licking at his bottom lip before taking it between her teeth and pulling on the flesh lightly. "I've been thinking about things, and I think we need to talk. Soon. We need to talk soon."

Scott nodded his head and pulled his head back to speak to the warm female that he was ready to strip and fuck on the sofa again. He stood and pulled her upright, holding her to steady her before he stepped away and walked slowly back to the desk to retrieve his cell phone. By the time he turned back to explain why he'd walked away, she was heading for the door.

"Stop. Lucy, you don't understand. I'm in as bad of shape as you are right now, you don't have to trust me, just look at me for chrissakes. My damn cock is hard enough to pound nails, but Randal had an accident, and he's in the hospital with a severe concussion. I promised Bolt that I'd bring you to the apartment so we could talk."

He ran his hand through his hair and shook off the remnants of sexual frustration. "I promised myself that the next time I got you naked, it would be in a bed. This is a hell of a time to test that resolve." He finally looked at her face and was surprised to see tears rolling down her cheeks. He grabbed up his cell phone and walked over to hug her. "Bolt says that Randal lost a lot of blood, but the doctor said that he'll be fine once the crack in his skull heals."

Scott told Aaron to tell Nicky and Laurie that Lucy was with him. The women were standing at their table yelling and waving dollar bills at the men on stage. Scott thought about that for a minute; why weren't they concerned about Lucy's whereabouts? Lucy didn't seem to be worried about them either.

In his experience, women traveled in packs. They usually went to the ladies room together; they checked make-up, compared nail polish, and when it came to watching men dancing for their pleasure, they would trample over their best friend to catch a G-string. He made a mental note to ask her about the strange behavior sometime.

It was too late for them to go to the hospital and see Randal, so Scott took Lucy back to the apartment. She didn't object, and while her silence during the ride caused him to wonder what was going through her mind, he decided to wait until he could pay attention to her without being distracted by driving in the heavy traffic of Friday night party goers.

Bolt was sitting in the living room when they walked into the apartment.

Lucy didn't believe that she'd ever seen a man that looked more miserable in her life. His hair was a mess, and his eyes were bloodshot. The tracks from his tears had dried on his handsome face, and she didn't hesitate to go to him where he sat. Bending over the hulking man was too awkward for her to maintain the position for more than a few seconds, so she bent her knees and sat on his lap. She pulled his head to her shoulder and hugged him as tightly as she could.

"Randal is a tough guy; we know that he'll be fine."

Watching her efforts to comfort Bolt made Scott fall in love with her just a little deeper. He kicked off his shoes and headed for the shower. He needed to get clean and get something to eat, in that order. Bolt was in good hands, so he left him in Lucy's tender care while he took care of his needs.

Lucy kept her hands moving as much as possible over Bolt's head and shoulders. Touch was something that she craved but had seldom received in her life. Her grandparents had not been cuddly types, but all three of the men that had inserted themselves into her life never walked out her door without a hug, and most times, a kiss.

Bolt wasn't crying, but he was squeezing her waist and hips to his body. On the way to the apartment, Scott had let it slip that he worried about Bolt.

"As far as I know, he hasn't given himself time to grieve for his parents. Now this accident that Randal had is just one more thing for him to keep bottled up. Bolt doesn't hesitate to let a person know that he cares, but he won't share any other kind of feelings."

Scott shook his hair from his eyes and glanced towards where she sat. "Men don't cry about things they can't change. They don't cry, and they don't whine about things that happen that they can't control. That's what our families raised each of us to believe. Men don't vent unless they are beating someone to a pulp, or engaging in some other manly occupation, like chopping wood or pounding nails into boards. We are supposed to channel our feelings into physical activity."

She remembered Scott's words. Men channel their feelings into physical activity, and since her thoughts were on the bulge under her right thigh, she grabbed two handfuls of Bolt's short hair and pulled his head up for an open mouthed kiss. She wasn't thinking about how the men would take it if she had sex with Bolt. She didn't care right at that minute. All she wanted was to make his hurt go away and maybe make the clench of need that she felt every time she came into contact with one of the men calm down a little bit.

Her fingers left his hair and traveled down to pull the shirt from his back. "I hope you don't have other plans for the night, but I need this, maybe you do too."

His head snapped up, and his eyes focused on hers. "This is not a good time to fuck with me. If you plan to stop this, do it now. I'm not in the mood to be tender and all the normal shit that goes with it. I want to bury my cock as deep as I can get and stay there until I can't move. If you don't want that, then get up and walk away now."

Her answer was a challenging grin, and her hands went to his belt buckle. "I'm finding out that I love the idea of seeing you so helpless that you can't move. I think I'm up for the challenge, big boy; I just hope that you aren't all talk and no action." She stood up before he could grab her. "Where's your room? If we're going to fuck until you can't move, I want something soft to lay on when we're done."

The world around her tilted upside down when he picked her up and tossed her over his shoulder, walking at a fast clip into the short hallway, and through the second door that they came to. The room was dark, but he didn't seem to need the light on to find the bed. He stood her on the mattress and worked the tight denim from her hips and thighs. Her panties came off with the jeans, and she heard him actually growl in frustration when the material bunched around her calves and kept her legs from spreading apart as he wanted them to. She held onto his shoulder and sat down with no grace or finesse. In fact, she plopped down on the softness of the bed and reached to untie her shoes.

She needn't have bothered to try untying them, Bolt pulled up one foot and then the other as he yanked the shoes off, and peeled the offensive material from her legs and feet.

There was no hesitation on his part, and though she should have been more cautious, she raised her hips to invite his touch.

"Let's see what you've got. You can see what I brought to the party; it's my turn."

He shook his head and sank a thick finger inside of her wet pink flesh. He added a second finger and worked the digits around, spreading them and sliding deeper until his fingers were as deep as they could go. She planted her feet and fucked herself on his fingers, demanding that he "hurry up and do something to help." She could hear the sound of his clothing hitting the floor before his hands pushed her bent knees further apart, and his body made the bed jostle as he climbed onto the mattress.

For a man that promised no tender lovemaking, he proved himself wrong as his fingertips ran up and down her inner thighs. She shivered and gasped when his body came down over hers, and his lips found her breast. The strength of the suction on her nipple was unbelievably pleasurable. The sharp sting of the nip of his teeth made her reach for him, but he straightened his back, and she felt his thickness entering her body. The initial stretch and retreat caused her to bend up to grab his shoulders. The deeper his cock went, the harder her fingers dug into his shoulders.

It wasn't painful, in fact, she loved the way his cock rubbed across the over sensitized nerve endings deep inside of her. The long slide out, followed by another long slide in didn't prepare her for sudden speed that his hips began to move with.

She held on and let him slam into her pussy again and again. He might be working his feelings out in a sexual way, but she was reaping the benefits of his coping mechanisms. The first tremors of an orgasm started, and she wrapped her legs around his back, locking her ankles together as their bodies moved in a choppy rhythm that brought each of them the pleasure they sought.

Lucy was almost climbing Bolt's body as the first orgasm strung her body into spasms and screams escaping from between her clenched teeth.

He slammed deep and stayed put while she ground herself up on his cock. He felt her fingernails in the flesh of his shoulders but didn't care. Her raised hips lifted his where they met, and he braced himself over her to give her everything that she needed to enjoy her orgasm to the fullest.

She quieted, and the clenching of her pussy lightened in intensity around his cock, so he pulled out of her body, smiling grimly when she whimpered at the loss. "Roll over onto your stomach, Lucy; there's a good girl." His hand ran over the soft skin of her back, and he urged her to widen her knees before he grasped her hips in his big hands and lined up his cock to reintroduce it to her hot, wet depths.

His hands pulled her back onto his prick, and he set a rhythm of fast, crisp jabs before lengthening his strokes to bury his cock until he could go no further inside of her body. Her cries were egging him on, combined with the renewed clenching of her inner muscles, and he moved with determination to work the rage of loss that was riding his soul. The physical exertion was welcomed, and he continued moving long after he shouted out his pleasure from the orgasm that her clenching body easily pulled from his cock.

He finally stopped the movement of his hips once his dick softened too much to stay inside of Lucy's body. His cock was so sensitive from the prolonged slamming through her tight cunt that he flinched. He hung over her back and laid his forehead between her shoulder blades while he caught his breath.

The whispered kiss that he gifted her skin with, caused her to shiver and smile. She crawled further up onto the bed and pulled the top covers back enough for her legs to slide underneath. She scooted down and raised her arm to hook his neck and bring it down towards her lips.

"Thank you for that. I enjoyed it more than I believed possible."

Her eyes closed before he could ask her if she was sore, or needed him to help her with a bath or something. As hard as it was for him to grasp, the woman fell asleep within seconds of getting comfortable. He shook his head and laughed quietly. It was no hardship for him to get up and pull the covers back on his side of the bed and join her sleeping body. He pulled her onto his chest and allowed her to grumble and re-arrange herself before he closed his eyes, at peace for the first time in days.

*****

Scott heard the two of them grunting and moaning as soon as he opened the bathroom door. He went into the living room and locked the door before heading to bed himself. He was tired, but not as tired as he'd been earlier. He walked towards his bedroom but didn't get any further than the open door of Bolt's room. He watched the lovers on the bed and felt his dick harden. He took himself in hand and jacked off while Bolt's silhouette showed on the wall behind the bed.

He was really working for that orgasm. Scott felt his balls tighten, ready to squirt and pulled the towel from his shoulder to keep from making a mess of the floor as he slumped against the doorjamb jerking his cock and groaning at the same time Bolt yelled his pleasure out loud.

Scott waited for a few long seconds, trying to force himself to go to his room. His feet didn't want to take him away from two of the people that he fully admitted to loving. He walked into the room and climbed in next to Lucy. He saw that Bolt was smiling, and it made him smile to know that Lucy had helped to put that peaceful look on his friend's face.

As he closed his eyes, he knew that the four of them would find a way to work out a life that included all of them. He had to have faith in the relationships that they had been building these past weeks. If one of them wasn't happy with the commitment, he wasn't certain what he would do.

He inched closer to her nude body, loving the feel of Lucy's warm flesh touching his skin. Too bad that she was asleep, because he wanted to make love with her and Bolt. It would wait for another time, but not too long. It took a while for his thoughts to calm down before he finally drifted to sleep.

Chapter 16

Randal woke up during the night twice with his skull feeling as if he'd been hit with a damn brick. He laid his thumb on the button to call the nurse each time and luckily enough, the squeak of the nurse's shoes was a welcome noise, even if it made him hold his head in an attempt to alleviate the pain stabbing behind his eyes.

The nurse checked his vitals and held up fingers for him to count. "Look, give me something to stop this pain or at least something to lighten the pain. My skull feels like a broken egg," he whispered. He kept his eyes closed while he did his best not to scream like a little girl. The scream was touch and go for the minute it took the nurse to inject his I.V. line with something to help ease the pounding.

The second time that he woke, he felt someone with their fingers on his wrist checking his pulse. Moving his head hurt, even moving his lips seemed to widen the cracks in his skull. He didn't try to open his eyes this time. He remembered the increased pain from opening his eyes even a slit the last time he woke up. "If you have another pain shot, now is a good time to use it, please." His hands gripped the bed rails to help him deal with the pain, but the shot was administered without argument.

The nurse had a nice voice. She spoke in a low tone, and he wished that he could tell her how much he appreciated her kindness. She pulled his eyelids open and checked his pupils, then continued her assessment. He heard her speaking, but couldn't understand what she was saying.

He was asleep before she left the room.

It was daylight when he woke for the third time. His hand was held down by someone's tight grip. He forced himself to open his eyes in narrow slits. Lucy was sitting next to his bed with his hand held in hers, and her head was laying against his thigh. She wasn't asleep; she was whispering to someone else in the room. He hated to interrupt her, but he needed a nurse and another one of those nice pain shots.

He returned the light grip of her fingers, and her head snapped up to look at his face. He blinked and tried to smile.

"Nurse, please, drink?"

Lucy frowned, but it took no time for her to hold a straw to his lips and once he swallowed a small sip, she took the refreshing liquid from him. She had hit the call button when she saw he was awake.

"I'm sorry. I know you're thirsty, and that your stomach is probably beginning to let you know that it wants to be fed. The doctor was in here earlier and said to limit your intake of food and liquids until the tests came back to tell us how bad the concussion is."

The nurse came into the room and held up her fingers, and they went through the protocol for severe concussions. The meds were wearing off fast, and he grunted when the nurse gently turned his head so she could take his temperature.

She apologized for his pain, "I'm so sorry for that, but it was either turn your head or climb over your body to reach the other ear. Considering that the I.V. and blood pressure clamp leads are over there, you got off easy. Doctor said to ease up on the meds a little. You won't be in pain, but this won't knock you out."

She flushed the I.V. before adding the pain medicine to the tube going into his vein and left him to Lucy's care. "He can have sips of water at a time, but don't give him too much, especially if he begins to feel nauseous. If he keeps the water down, we might be able to give him some broth or jello. He will be on a clear liquid diet today, and it will be up to the doctor if he can have anything solid tomorrow."

Lucy looked to the corner of the room and smiled at Scott. He was sacked out in the chair by the window. She only felt a small tinge of guilt for waking the men up this morning at five AM. She was just so used to waking up early to get ready for work. They'd grumbled when she'd crawled over the foot of the bed to leave their warmth. Her thighs were sticky, and she needed a shower. Remembering how her thighs got that way

made her smile while the water sluiced over her skin.

She had a pot of coffee brewing and was munching on a bowl of Randal's favorite granola cereal when Bolt came into the room. He grinned at her and poured himself a cup of the dark roast. She brought the empty bowl to the sink next to where he stood and reached for a mug in the cupboard.

Bolt set his cup down and pulled her into his embrace. His lips locked on hers, and they were both breathing heavy when he drew back and reached for the coffee pot to fill the cup that she still had dangling from her fingers. He'd taken the mug and set it on the table where she had been sitting before filling it and putting the pot back. He leaned down over her shoulder once Lucy sat down, to whisper, "Thank You," in her ear.

She knew that she blushed, but she didn't feel embarrassed about what they'd done last night. She smiled at his look of surprise when she told him, "It was my pleasure. Believe me; anytime you feel the need for a repeat, just ask." She laughed when his eyebrow arched up.

"I don't know what it is about you guys, but every time I'm around one or two of you, my inner slut seems to want to take over." She shook her head, puzzled over the things that she'd just told him. Admitting her new desires should have, at least, given her enough reason to leave before she blurted out the secret yearning for the men that she held as close to her heart as she dared. She wanted them to love her, even knowing that she was such a greedy woman didn't stop the wanting.

Common sense and fear of what they would do and say kept her from laying it all out this morning. Scott wandered into the room, and Bolt waited until he was seated to explain what had happened the night before.

"I came home because Lucy stood me up last night. I walked in and knew something was off." His eyes looked haunted when he said, "I thought he was dead. There was so much blood, and he was- he was wedged between the toilet and the tub." He took a minute to drink his coffee and compose himself.

"I cleaned up the mess, but I'll be damned if we live here much longer. I'm going house hunting today. We need room to move around, and this place was only supposed to be temporary to begin with. Randal could have died if I hadn't found him, and it took just about everything I had to try to move him so the paramedics could get to him."

She sat without saying anything. The men were listing what they needed for their comfort. Things like room sizes and bathrooms were all well and good, necessary even, but she hoped they realized that they would need room for entertaining and for a home office. She might offer some suggestions later on, once they found a few houses that they were seriously thinking about buying.

She wondered why they were buying a house together. Unless her suspicions were correct, and if that was the case, it made perfect sense for them to buy a big home. She knew that she wasn't the most observant person in the world, but she'd swear that these men enjoyed more than a close friendship. They looked at each other with more than affection, and her heart wanted them to look at her the same way they did one another.

Just the thought of watching these beautiful men making love to one another made her breath catch. The thought of watching them licking and sucking... Good grief, she had to redirect her thoughts or she might demand to see them strip down right here in the kitchen. She didn't even want to think about what they would say or do if she was mistaken.

They were all young enough to have families of their own, and she doubted if too many women would get along well enough to actually live in the same house together with the other men and their possible families. Not that she was an expert at getting along with people. Working at the company was different than living with someone. She shrugged, *Not your decision girlie; you are just using these gorgeous men as sex objects, right?*

The thought made her smile sadly. She was already more than halfway in love with each of them. She couldn't risk her feelings getting any deeper. They were separate but seemed like a packaged deal.

Scott drove them to the hospital, and he claimed the chair in the corner to finish his sleep. She pulled the bedside chair closer and waited for Randal to wake up. She studied his bruised face and decided that he didn't look as bad as she was sure he felt. He was moaning in his sleep, and she hissed at Scott, trying to get his attention to send him for the nurse. Randal had awoken before Scott opened his eyes, so she pulled her hand away from his and pressed the call button to summon the nurse.

*****

Randal was happy to be home. He'd spent most of the past week in the hospital, and was still feeling like hell. The best part about laying in that hospital were the visits from Lucy. The guys were great; they were doing their best to keep him company and make the hours more tolerable.

He wasn't used to laying around. She came to keep him company almost every day, and he enjoyed the way she taunted him when she knew what the crossword puzzle clues meant before he did. He found that reading was difficult for any length of time; he must have told her at some point because the next day she surprised him by bringing an E-reader with her so that he could listen to his choice of several books that she had on hand.

It was a handy item to have, and he thanked her with an open mouthed kiss. That kiss cost him in discomfort and pain, but she was worth it. The earbuds kept the day to day noise from interrupting the voice reading the latest best-selling Mystery novel.

Scott and Bolt had made sure that he had everything he might need before they left for the day. He was now sitting in the living room in front of the television, with a huge glass of water and one filled with sweet iced tea. The snacks were on the table, but he hadn't had much of an appetite since the accident. He closed his eyes and daydreamed while the talk show host succeeded in pissing off his guest enough to have the man storm off of the stage amidst the boos of the audience.

He was still taking pain meds for the headaches, but the stuff that they sent him home with was not nearly as effective as the shots had been. He had to try to redirect his thoughts to keep from dwelling on the dull throbbing in his head. The stabbing "ice pick to the brain" pains were the worst. But this stuff gave him the same buzz that a few too many whiskey shots did.

"Who'd of thought one little pill could make the room spin. I'll be damned."

He must have dozed off, because the next thing he knew, Lucy was brushing the hair away from his closed eyelids. He knew it was her; he could smell the soap that she used. It was a scent that he would forever more associate with the pretty woman with blonde hair and blue eyes. If what he felt wasn't love, it had to be pretty damn close. He loved Bolt and Scott and knew that they loved him equally.

Lucy brought something altogether different to his soul. She calmed him, made him think about any subject before he spoke, and she didn't hold back from teasing the hell out of him if she could find an excuse. He opened his eyes and watched the slight frown on her face turn to a smile, as she noticed he was watching her.

"I'm so happy that they let you go home. I know the guys have to be excited to not have to run up to the hospital every day. Not that it's a chore or anything, and seeing you getting better each day was worth all of the running."

She stopped talking for a second and shrugged. "I'm sorry, I got so excited to see that you're home and upright in a chair. It's almost like you're completely well. I've been worried you know."

She was too sweet, and he wanted her. The earlier dizziness was gone, and the slight throb in his head was pushed aside to make room for thinking that he wanted those pouty lips wrapped around his cock. He reached for the glass of water to wet his dry mouth. She was watching him, and he smiled.

Lucy wondered what was wrong with Randal. He had an odd look in his eyes, and she felt a little like he might have been stalking

her. If he was mobile and she was moving that was. The thought made her grin at him.

"You look like a cat waiting for the mouse to show up. Do you need something?"

His low laugh and hand reaching out to snag her arm should have clued her into his intentions of pulling her down to sit on his lap. He nuzzled her neck and gave the pulse under her earlobe a slow lick, followed by a soft kiss. His lips and tongue continued to navigate the skin of her neck and the cradle of her collar bone. His words sounded husky, but the request that he made was not a big surprise. The thick roll of his cock was resting on his upper thigh under the cheek of her ass.

"You want to know what I need? I need those beautiful lips wrapped around my cock. Can you do me that little favor?" His fingers teased the tips of her nipples that were quickly hardening and begging for attention. "I was dreaming of watching your mouth sucking my cock, and when I opened my eyes, there you were."

Lucy thought about his request. She didn't dwell on the idea, just slid from his lap and knelt between his long legs. She pulled the light blanket back and saw that he was wearing cartoon pajama pants with the white t-shirt. The head of his cock was peeking out between the button fly.

She smiled into Randal's narrowed eyes, and teased, "It looks like you have a problem here." She leaned down and gave the dark pink skin a slow lick.

She had to smile even as she shook her head and reached to free him from the buttoned material that appeared to be tight enough to leave a ring impressed into the fleshy knot of nerves under the head of his cock. The way he sucked in a breath made her grab both sides of the material above the constricted muscle and yanked it apart. The button was lost when it snapped off. Her hands ringed his cock and he moaned.

She massaged the soft skin covering the hard thick flesh. "You really have a beautiful cock you know. Not that I've seen that many until I met you and Scott, and now that I've seen Bolt's cock, I have to say I'm impressed." Her hands were rubbing, and her fingers were pinching the skin of his shaft and the spot where his balls and cock met.

"I'm finding out things about myself that I never dreamed I might want." She leaned down and licked the head all around before she slowly suctioned the head into her mouth, all the while looking up at his face to see him watching her. His clenched jaw let her know that he was paying attention. And when her hand let go of its hold on his cock and pinched the skin under his ballsack, he groaned as if he was in pain. His head fell back to rest on the pillowed cushion on the back of the chair, and his hands were tightly gripping the armrests of the thickly cushioned seat.

She gave up checking for his reactions and concentrated on giving him the orgasm that he'd asked her for. She hummed and ran her tongue around the small slit in the center of the head of his cock. She could feel the pulse beginning in his shaft under her fingers even before she felt his cock readying itself on her tongue. His fist hit the armrest as he yelled and twisted his hips as his orgasm took over and she did her best to ride it out with half of his cock enjoying the warm wetness of her mouth and lips.

When his body stopped moving, she drew back from his softening cock and wiped the excess cream from her cheeks and chin on the lightweight blanket near his hip. There had been no way to contain the entirety of his cum, especially with the way he moved in such jerky movements.

She didn't realize that something was wrong until she heard a shout from behind her and felt the hands reaching under her arms to pull her back from Randal's legs. She came up from the place she'd been set, swinging her fist. It connected with the back of Scott's knee, and he went down, barely avoiding landing on top of Randal's now writhing body.

Bolt was checking Randal's eyes and trying to keep the man's hands from grabbing his head in response to the pain that slammed into his brain just as he began to orgasm.

Scott was crushing a pill between two teaspoons, and he added a small amount of water to half of the white powder. He pulled Randal's bottom lip out and pressed down. "Open your mouth buddy; this will work quick. It'll taste like shit, but it's all we've got."

Lucy sat on the floor wondering what just happened. Bolt had gone to the kitchen and came back with an ice pack that he put behind Randal's neck, and Scott was rubbing his neck to keep the medicine from gagging him.

"Come on, man, swallow it back. Try to imagine it's Bolt's cum; you know how sour his semen is, right? You have Lucy scared to death over here, and now you'll play merry hell talking her into sucking your cock ever again." He kept fussing over the big man until he could see his breathing become easier, and his skin lost the putty color around his cheeks and mouth. He stepped back and looked for Bolt.

The door was open, and neither Bolt nor Lucy was standing in the room with him and Randal. He wanted to follow the two that were missing but decided to stay with Randal. He wasn't out of pain yet, and Scott had confidence in Bolt's abilities to talk to Lucy. They'd walked through the front door to see Lucy on her knees between Randal's thighs, and were enjoying the sights and sounds until Randal started jerking around and they saw his eyes roll back.

They'd returned from viewing a house that had almost everything that was on the wish list. The place had been nice, but the room sizes wouldn't work for them. There were several more homes to view in the coming week, but they hadn't ruled out building a home. The idea was a favorite choice for Scott, but Bolt wanted something immediate instead of being forced to wait for contractors and permits.

They decided on the ride home this afternoon that it was past time they spoke with Lucy about the possibility of her joining them to form the family that the three friends craved. Scott agreed. It had been two months since they'd found her, and she should have some idea as to what she felt for the men that had pushed themselves into her life like they had purposefully done. It was time that they got everything out and on the table.

Lucy watched as Bolt and Scott worked over Randal, and it scared the hell out of her. She'd hurt Randal and hadn't even realized what had happened until it might be too late.

"How was I supposed to know that something as simple as a blow job would kill him? I need to go home and stay there. This is not going to work; you know that. Hell, Lucy, what were you thinking to let him talk you into it."

Bolt followed her out the door and heard her berating herself. He wanted to smile at the ridiculous assumption that she'd almost killed Randal.

"Lucy, I need to talk to you for a few minutes before you run home and lock the door." He caught her off guard when he interrupted her lecture, and she stopped walking for the quick second that it took for him to reach out for the hand that was waving around while she was talking to herself. He turned her towards him by pulling gently on her hand.

"He isn't dead or dying; Randal just has a bad headache." Bolt held her shoulders and bent down to look into her beautiful eyes that were drowning in tears. "What you don't know is that he would want your lips on his body even if he was on his death bed. You don't

realize that we all feel the same." He gave her shoulders a slight shake and slowly walked her back to the apartment as he spoke. "For a smart woman, you sure lack confidence in yourself."

He led her through the door and closing it behind them. "Come on; we need to talk and since we're all here in one place, now is as good a time as any."

Randal was still in the chair where they'd left him. He was awake, but he was rolling his head back and forth on the ice pack under his neck, and laughing quietly. Scott was in the kitchen ordering Chinese take out for their dinner.

Bolt grinned at her. "See? Everything is right and tight in the world."

Scott joined them in the doorway to the living room and grinned at the sight of Randal enjoying the high that the powerful painkiller was giving him. He turned to Bolt and shrugged as he pulled Lucy into a tight embrace. "From what I can understand, he saw our Lucy and remembered how pretty those lips," the punch to his gut made the words stop in his throat. Lucy stepped from his arms and stomped his foot for good measure.

"I'm right here; you don't get to talk about me as if I can't hear you or what you're saying about me isn't my business." She tossed her head up and gave the two men in front of her a narrow-eyed look.

Pointing at Bolt, she said, "You wonder why I have no confidence? It's because of people that seem to think that because I don't shove them aside to get attention or be heard that I don't have an opinion, that I don't matter. I matter. I can make decisions, and sometimes I screw up, but I'm a human." She turned her back on the surprised men and walked over to where Randal sat. He had stopped rolling his head and appeared to be paying attention to what she was saying.

"You are in trouble, mister. If I hadn't come back and seen you laughing like a lunatic, I would have still been thinking that I killed you. If you weren't still hurt, I would kick you for scaring me like that." She shook her finger at him. "Don't ask me to do that again."

She couldn't deal with anymore tonight. Bolt told her that they needed to talk, and she knew that he was right, but tonight was not the night. She needed to think, and she couldn't do that with one or all of them hovering over her head while she tried to sort it out. The strange references to the taste of Bolt's semen and several other hints that flooded her brain made her look at the men in turn while the thoughts processed in her mind. She needed to ask a few questions to clarify what she was thinking about.

"I have a few questions, and I want truthful answers, please." She waited for the resigned look on Bolt's face and the sober but determined look on Scott's face, and the nods of their heads before she asked her questions.

"Are you guys bisexual? Has the way you've been paying attention to me been for some reason other than looking for an easy piece of ass? I mean, I've made it pretty obvious that I am attracted to each of you; which, by the way, has more to do with your personalities than anything else. The physical stuff is a bonus."

She stood with her arms folded waiting for them to answer. Randal was beginning to snore behind her, and she didn't blame him. She was dead tired herself. Bolt stepped forward, but she held her hand out to stop him from approaching her.

He detoured to the couch and sat down with a sigh. He kicked his shoes off and lifted his feet to rest on the table in front of him. Scott turned away to answer the door and brought back a large bag of delicious smelling food. He sat it on the table by Bolt's feet, and the feet dropped to the floor quickly.

She was ignored while Scott walked to the kitchen to bring back bottles of beer, plates and forks. He looked at her when he shoved the ottoman to the opposite side of the table for her to sit on. "We don't use chopsticks, the only one of us that can manipulate the damn things is Randal, and he's not in any shape to use even a sippy cup right now."

She could walk out, or she could sit down and eat and hope that her questions got answered before she left to go home tonight. She sat down and accepted the paper plate and fork that were handed to her, and filled her plate.

It wasn't until the cartons were almost empty, and the beer in front of her was substituted for a cola, that the men began to give her the answers that she wanted.

Bolt leaned forward with his elbows resting on his knees. She could see that he was gathering his words, and appreciated that they were taking her questions seriously enough to try to answer them.

"I guess that we don't try very hard to hide the way that the three of us feel about each other. Our families know that we are more than friends, but most people have no idea, and while we aren't ashamed of our lifestyle, some people get preachy, and some are pretty hostile." He looked at Scott and shrugged.

"Some people think that we have to be one or the other; it never worked that way for me. I know for a fact that Scott got in more than a few fights with his family members over his sexuality. And Randal, well Randal has grandparents that want him married, and they went so far as to offer me and Scott a large amount of cash to leave Randal alone.

"I always hear that we don't choose who we will fall in love with, but I don't believe that. I have loved these guys since we were in junior high and the football coach tried to molest a cheerleader in the boys locker room after a game. The girl came from a poor family, and the school wasn't going to make him accountable. However, they didn't want the bad press if it got out that he molested three members of his football team. He'd never touched us, not once, but we stuck together, and he got put in a place where he couldn't hurt anyone again. He died sitting in prison. We've been inseparable since. The sex just happened naturally. Kids experiment, and when they are as lucky as the three of us were, the bond forms so tight that nothing can break it."

He wiped his face with the napkin that he still held in his hand.

Scott began talking next, and she listened. So far every word that Bolt had said sounded truthful and legitimate.

"You already know that we enjoy sex with women. We've talked about it, and not one of us like men better than sex with women; it's pretty much equal."

Randal spoke, interrupting Scott, and making them all stare at him as his crude wording sank in.

"What they are trying to say to you is that we like fucking women, correction, we like fucking you. One of these days, we'll take turns eating your pretty little pussy, and you can decide who is better at it. I, for one, am planning to make you the middle of a sandwich." He made a snorting noise and closed his eyes, but he kept talking. "I can see it now, Bolt laying on the bottom buried in your little asshole; me laying between your legs, licking your pussy while looking up to see those fuck me lips of yours wrapped around Scott's dick. So fucking hot."

His mouth stayed open a little as he started snoring again; Scott laughed softly. Randal was doped up and still had a bad concussion, but that didn't stop him from giving his opinion. It was great. Lucy looked confused but interested in what Randal said.

She looked back at the two men that made her heart flutter every time she thought about them for more than a minute at a time.

"How exactly do I fit into this family that you guys have formed? I mean, I can tell that you appreciate women and sex with women too. Why me? And how can a relationship like what this sounds like it might become work? I can't walk into a situation like this without thinking about the consequences. I want a family; maybe a child or two. I can't find someone to settle down with if I'm always available for you guys when you're in the mood for a booty call.

"I won't deny it; ever since the night of my birthday, you guys have held my attention. I can count on two fingers of one hand how many men have taken up so much of my time for more than a week or two. To go from being plain me, to suddenly being the sex object to three of the sexiest men in the county is hard to accept. It's even harder to accept that I want to have sex with all of you."

Bolt was shaking his head as she talked. "I asked you how an intelligent woman like yourself could be so dense earlier today. This is the way it is; we want you to join our circle, be our woman; our only woman. We want a mother for our children, but we could hire a surrogate for birthing babies if it's not something you want to do. A surrogate won't be around to love a child or kiss their scrapes and tuck them in at night when we aren't there some nights. I have to travel at times for the company. Randal has to travel once or twice a year, and Scotty here, he goes to motorcycle rallies.

"We can adjust our lives to accommodate children; God knows they would be more than welcome. We want a woman that has a huge heart with love to share; enough love to love and care for a big family. We think that you are that woman."

He didn't try to continue to convince her of their intentions. Scott nodded his head when she glanced his way, but he kept quiet and rubbed the foot that was propped on his knee. It was the foot that she had stomped on earlier. She closed her eyes and breathed deeply through her nose. She needed to think about this, and she needed to be alone to do it. She stood up and walked into the kitchen to grab her purse from the table where she'd left it, then walked back to the men in the living room.

"Thank you for being honest with me. I have a lot to think about, and I promise that I'll let you know what I've decided as soon as I can."

She gave each man a long look and turned to look at Randal sleeping in the chair. "Take care of him, and you guys stay out of trouble."

Chapter 18

It had been ten days since she'd seen any of the men. She had gone through her day to day routines and spent her evenings daydreaming, masturbating in the bathtub, and watching sappy "chick flicks" for a reason to allow herself to cry.

Something that she had never done was go through the boxes that were in the closet. The items belonged to her grandparents. She was surprised to see so many baby pictures and wondered who the two children that sat with her at a table with a birthday cake in front of her highchair were. They must be cousins or neighbors from her earliest years because she didn't remember them or any other kids other than classmates from her childhood.

There were pictures of a young couple wearing old-fashioned clothes, and it was obvious that the day was their wedding day from the small bouquet of flowers held tightly in the girl's grasp. She was also very pregnant if the puffed ruffle of the shirt she wore was any indication. The man was tall and slender. He had dark brown hair, and his eyes appeared to be brown, but it was difficult to see their exact color because of the poor quality of the photograph.

The girl in the picture was blonde and on the shorter side from the appearance of her head barely clearing the man's shoulder. Lucy tried to reconcile the features of the two in the photo with her own facial structure, but she could find no resemblance.

Aside from the pictures, there were handwritten journals dating back to the nineteen thirties, and several papers that were stamped with an embossed seal; some were dated two months after she was born. Her disability caused frustration to set in each time she tried to decipher the words in the legal papers. The journals were completely hopeless. She could make out several words that were typewritten, but the handwriting was put aside without a thought. She wanted to know what the documents meant but didn't know who to take them to without opening herself to ridicule.

There was a small box filled with jewelry and trinkets that she could see a young woman treasuring. There was a leather string purse with old coins and a roll of old dollar bills with the coins, so she set the bag aside while she dug further into the boxes. Her grandfather's watch was sitting on the dresser where her grandmother had left it, but there was another watch in a small case. It looked brand new, as if it had never been out of the velvet covered cardboard box that it came in.

The clothing was all old but in good shape. They smelled musty, but after she went through everything and found nothing in the pockets or the box, she placed them carefully back and put the lid on the vintage clothes. What she would do with all of this stuff was a mystery. The box of papers and pictures kept drawing her eyes, and she spent hours looking at the photos and trying to understand what the pictures could tell her.

By day fifteen, she was ready to give the men her decision. Everything she owned including the clues to her parent's whereabouts was in the stack of boxes to be loaded into the moving truck waiting in her driveway. The men had better not have changed their minds because she had just turned the house over to the Senior housing authority. Once she made her decision, the rest of her planning fell into place.

She left the furniture because it was still in good shape and if it wasn't needed, the people in the neighborhood could sell it at the annual rummage they held in the spring.

Her letter of resignation had been mailed this morning on the way to work. She was throwing her lot in with blind trust and all she hoped for was that the men would be ready for the total commitment that she was ready to bring to the relationship.

She tossed an overnight bag into the back seat of the sedan and cranked the radio up so she wouldn't try to talk herself out of this move. She had been solitary most of her life, and now she had the opportunity to be allowed to hug and touch people. The opportunity to probably have children to shower with all of the love that she had been holding inside for so long. The best part was that she would never be alone. She would never have to live with silence unless she wanted it that way.

Knowing that there were three handsome men that wanted her to be theirs gave her the shivers; remembering how they showed her that they wanted her, well those memories had kept her awake many nights over the past two weeks. She loved them. There was no doubt in her mind. When just the thought of living on her own still, and not accepting the men gave her such a feeling of grief, she knew that she would be theirs.

****

The men were getting into Randal's double cab pick-up when she pulled into the driveway behind Scott's little red sports car. Bolt was still standing on the concrete of the drive, so he came over to where she sat in her car, and opened her door.

"We're heading over to see a house that Randal found while he was recuperating. He swears that this is the home for us. Why don't you come along and give us your opinion of the place?"

She grabbed her purse and the keys from the ignition and let him pull her up and out of the car. His arms came around her in a close hug, and her feet left the ground as he held onto her and walked to the truck to set her on the seat next to Scott. She was laughing as Scott pulled the seat belt over her shoulder.

"I wasn't going to run off you know. I came over to let you know what I decided. I decided that we should try to make this family work; that is if you guys still want me to be here, with you, I mean."

The speech that she had planned to make when she was with them was so messed up that she shut her mouth to avoid making a fool of herself.

Scott reached out and snagged her hand, bringing it to his lips for a whisper soft kiss. "We heard your car coming down the block, and it was all we could do to act like it was no big deal. We have an appointment to see this house that Randal found, but when we get back home, we can talk. Really talk."

She joined them in the nods of agreement. It could wait, and she began to look forward to seeing this house that Randal started telling her about while he drove.

She was impressed when they pulled into the driveway and stopped in front of a brick Colonial with overgrown bushes hiding the front windows and a large black and white cat that didn't bother to raise his head as they walked up to the front door.

The place was not a neighborhood showcase type of home. A person didn't have to look past the cracks in the sidewalk to know that a family had lived here. The thought that the house needed a new family, and someone to love it made her smile at Randal. His choice of house was a good one. There would be repairs that were necessary, but they could paint the rooms and fill in cracks. The place felt like home before she even stepped foot inside.

The feline was lounging on one of the flower tables by the entranceway, and Lucy reached out to give him a scratch. Kitty raised his head and stood up. He studied her just as intently as she was staring at him, but when she reached to pick him up, he snubbed her. Kitty jumped down and disappeared into the bushes.

The realtor opened the front door, and they stepped into the foyer. Anyone could see that the house had been lived in. As they wandered through the spaces, she could picture a family living here. The huge family room had a fireplace and built-in bookshelves, and the kitchen was in serious need of updating, but Lucy loved it.

The only thing about the house that bothered her was the small, light yellow and baby blue room situated through a door leading from the master bedroom. The balloons and bears decorating the walls made her think of the baby that she lost. She hung back while the rest followed the realtor.

She walked around the little room and could see the indents in the carpeting where the legs of a crib had been sitting. The closet door was ajar, and she didn't resist opening it further. She stopped in her tracks when she saw the small pile of toys that had been shoved into a cotton carry bag. A stuffed lion that was missing most of its yarn mane was lying half out of the bag. The little pillow with a toy dump truck embroidered on the widest panel was visible too.

She tried to leave the nursery. She told herself that she was being ridiculous, but the next thing she knew, she was sitting next to the bag.

The men found her sitting on the floor with the old lion between her hands, and she was crying as if her heart was broken.

The realtor was standing by the stairs when they came down the steps with Bolt carrying Lucy's exhausted body. Her arms hung around his neck, and little eep noises escaped her mouth while she tried to stop the misery that held her in its grip.

Randal assured the woman that everything was fine, that Lucy was not feeling well and that they would need to reschedule.

Bolt didn't bother sitting her in a seat by herself. He placed her on the back seat of the truck and climbed inside on the other side, before pulling her into his arms and laying his head next to hers. He needed to let her know that he was there and felt her pain, but wasn't going to leave her alone.

The drive back to the apartment was silent. No one wanted to talk about Lucy's emotional state until they were where the long overdue discussion could take place.

Randal pulled into the driveway, got out of the truck and opened the back passenger door to take Lucy from Bolt's lap. He didn't bother to set her on her feet; instead, he cradled her in his arms and walked to the door that Scott was holding wide open.

Lucy sat on the couch without knowing what to say to the men that had treated her so tenderly more than once. How something as small as a child's forgotten toy could turn her into a crying mess was crazy, but it happened. She finally drew a deep breath and looked up to see the men staring at her with varying degrees of concern.

"I am so sorry. I'm never that weak, but since the attack and the doctor telling me that I had lost the baby, a baby I was too stupid to admit to myself was inside of me-" She had to stop speaking for a few seconds to gulp back the self-pitying sobs. "I loved that house, I really did, but the nursery triggered this sorrow that is so deep inside of me that I have no control over it. I saw that toy and the pillow, and wondered if the baby I carried had been a boy or a girl."

"That is a family home." She looked up and directly into Bolt's eyes. "I came here this morning to see if we could maybe make a relationship between the four of us work. I feel like I ruined your day." She looked at each man in turn, and they all shook their heads.

Scott smiled and came over the table with his long legs stretching and over balanced to land next to her where she watched him with her mouth hanging open. The laugh slipped from her throat, and it startled her. She put her fingertips to her lips and watched Scott straightening up enough to lean over and stared into her eyes as he nibbled at the fingers that were in his way.

"You need to lower those little fingers; I want to kiss you, and I want those hands holding on tight digging into my back."

Randal laughed, remembering the bloody mess those little fingers left the last time she'd held on tight. Thankfully, it appeared that she had cut her nails. He relaxed and smiled at Bolt.

Chapter 19

Lucy found herself naked within minutes as the men pulled her clothes from her body. She had been busy pulling the shirts from their shoulders, and her hands had been exploring one naked chest after the other.

Bolt's fingers slid between the soaked lips of her pussy, and she moved her hips to push his digits deeper inside. Randal had his hands filled with her breasts, and her nipples appreciated the attention that his fingertips gave them. The light pinching and pulling was driving her wild, and making her excitement ramp up.

How they knew exactly what she needed and wanted didn't matter to her. She wanted to make them feel as good as they made her feel, but once Bolt pulled her legs around his head that was on the couch cushions, she was on all fours. His long, slow lick started at her clit and ended somewhere in the middle of the crease of her ass. His fingers continued to penetrate her while his lips sucked the tiny muscle of her clit between his teeth and she gasped.

Scott held her jaw in his palm, and she nuzzled his hand before he raised her head enough to offer her lips his cock. She raised her eyes and licked her bottom lip before taking the dark pink flesh inside of her mouth.

She felt the gentle pulse of his heartbeat on her bottom lip and ran her tongue over her teeth to give his cock a gentle lick.

She began to steadily suck harder as she pulled more of his meat into the heat of her throat. She gagged herself and had to draw back until the discomfort stopped. His hand used pressure on her head to force her to take more of his length, and she scraped the sensitive skin of his shaft with her teeth. He backed off with the pushing, and she smiled as she took another half inch of him inside as a reward for knowing when to back off.

The fingers in her pussy were going deeper, and she couldn't help but pump her hips faster. When he pulled his fingers out of her, leaving her empty, she moaned in frustration around the cock in her mouth which triggered his orgasm. She drew back and took a deep breath before pushing down on Scott's cock and taking him as deep as she could while he flooded her throat with his liquid offering.

Slick fingers startled her as she felt a finger push into her asshole. Ever since the possibility of being with three men at the same time had been on her list of favorite fantasies, she wondered how it would feel to have something as large as a man's cock in her smallest opening. She held her breath for a minute and let it out slowly. That finger had been joined by another, and she could feel the stretch. There was some discomfort, but within a few strokes of his slick digits, her opening had gotten used to the feeling of fullness.

Between the lips and fingers teasing the wet depths of her pussy, and the slippery fingers shuttling in and out of her asshole, she couldn't remain still or silent. Her vaginal muscles clamped down on Bolt's fingers, and she ground her clit on his chin on each down-stroke of her pumping hips. She gasped for breath and hung her head, trying to gather her scattered senses. "Holy fuck, this feels so good, don't stop."

Randal lined his cock up at the small starburst of her asshole and slowly began to penetrate the tightest place he'd ever stuck his dick in. His hands pulled the cheeks of her ass apart, and he enjoyed watching his cock slide into her hot body. "That is so beautiful. Your ass is perfect for this. You're squeezing my cock so damned tight that I want to blow, but I want to make this ride last a bit longer."

He leaned over her back and placed his hands over her dangling breasts. "Here we go, kitten, let's bring you up so you can let Bolt bury his cock in your pretty pussy." He pulled her upright, and she slid further down on his thick cock. "Oh, that's incredible. If you relax a little bit, the discomfort will ease, honey. I just hope I can last long enough to give you a chance to enjoy this."

Her head fell back onto Randal's shoulder, and when she looked down, she saw something that fascinated her. It almost took the stinging from Bolt's teeth scraping her clit, but the tremors that were starting to take hold of her body could not be denied for more than the few seconds it took her to slam her ass back on the cock in her back entrance, while she ground her pussy on Bolt's fingers and tongue.

She could not take her eyes off of the sight of Scott sucking strongly on Bolt's cock. His hair hid most of her view of the cock shaft sliding into his mouth, but he raised his eyes to hers once he had Bolt's cock deep into his throat and began pulling back , only to slide back down. He worked his jaw sideways, and she felt the groan that Bolt made vibrating on her clit from his lips. Scott winked at her and raised one hand to play with the nipple of her left breast that hung just above Randal's hand where he held her body upright.

That pinch and the long slide of the thick cock in her ass gliding over the sensitive nerves that she never knew were buried so deep inside, caused her to jerk and enjoy as the pulse of her orgasm take control of her body. She screamed her release and felt Randal's cum flooding into the tip of the condom. Every nerve ending responded by clenching down on his cock and making him twitch and wrap his arms completely around her body to hold her in place while he did his best to calm his breathing.

Scott's head bobbed up and down faster. She could see Bolt's hips raise and felt every sound that he made as he shouted against her soaked flesh. Another small orgasm jerked her stiff, and she cried out while Randal held her from falling on top of Scott.

It took a few minutes for everyone to calm down, and untangle from each other, but Lucy laughed once she was placed on her feet and immediately sat on Bolt's stomach. He hadn't been quick enough to sit up, and her legs were so shaky that she sat down before falling down. The breath was knocked out of him, but he took the assault well. Seeing his face glistening with the creamy juice from her pussy, stopped her laughter, and she leaned down to kiss him.

She tasted herself on his lips, but other than a salty tinge, she didn't think about it. Knowing that he made no demands, just gave her pleasure, made her heart melt even more. These men were her men. Yes, she liked that; her men. Now they just needed to make sure everyone would be happy and committed to the relationship.

Seeing the men all relaxed and naked without anyone scrambling for covering made her feel like they trusted her, so she forced herself not to jump up and run to find her clothes. She crawled over Bolt and laid her head on Scott's thigh, raising her legs to stretch them out over Randal's lap. She fell asleep for a few minutes and woke to find herself being carried into the bathroom for a much-needed shower.

Randal was finishing a phone call when Lucy walked into the kitchen the next morning. She'd slept in Bolt's arms all night, and the scent of freshly brewed coffee pulled her from his warm embrace to walk into the kitchen for a cup.

She added a splash of milk to the cup and winced a little when she sat on the hard wooden seat of the kitchen chair. Randal smiled and patted his leg.

"You can sit on my lap if you aren't comfortable. I know that we put you through quite a workout last night."

She knew that she was blushing. This was the man that had gone where no one or thing had ever gone before, and she knew that it would happen again. Maybe not with him right away, but with either of the other men it was bound to happen, and if last night was any measure of things to come, she might request having her ass filled.

"It's sad really; every time I'm around you men, my common sense takes a hike, and all that's left is a nymphomaniac. What is it about you guys that makes me want to jump your bones, but at the same time, I'm dying of curiosity to see you loving each other. Watching Scott go down on Bolt was so hot that I came even though Bolt bit me."

She didn't look away from his face as she spoke, and he was smiling before she was finished speaking. "Yes, I know, I talk out loud too much, but you guys have driven me to distraction more than once."

Randal laughed. "I just bought that house; I figure that we can do most of the painting and stuff. We will have to add a detached garage, but it should be comfortable enough for us to live in if you are here to give us a chance to show you that we value you more than you will ever find from anyone else.

"I can't promise you that you will never be sad, or that I won't piss you off from time to time. Truthfully, all I can promise you is my loyalty and all of the love that you will accept from me." His face was solemn when he reached for her hand. "Can you promise me the same? Can you find enough room in your heart for three men and any children that might come from that love?"

She looked around when she heard steps coming into the room behind where she sat. Love hadn't been mentioned much, just once or twice in passing. She knew that she had been sunk within the week that she had been released from the hospital. That fantasy of being loved by all three of the men was coming to life and she wondered aloud.

"What if I'm not enough? You guys, well, look at you. I'm not a troll, but you don't see men that look like you do with women like me. I can't read well. I don't have a lot of money to bring into this deal. All I have is me and a truckload of boxes that will be here around

noon. I don't know if I could lose you all if you decide that I'm not enough for you."

Randal and Scott shook their heads while Bolt scowled.

Randal finally spoke, and what he said made sense.

"Yeah, look at us. Men like us who've been chased by the cheerleaders, the prom queens and the medically enhanced beauties that have egos as big as their silicone breast implants." He shrugged his wide shoulders, and looked at Bolt and Scott in turn, before continuing.

"I won't lie to you; we have together, and separately, done a good bit of chasing and feeling like the big deals once we conquered the beauty queens and such. The need to fuck anything that other men worshiped got old damn fast. Those beauty queens need constant reassurance that they are the prettiest, the sexiest, the best." His hands raised and lowered as he talked, and Scott took up the conversation.

"He's not saying that we don't think you're beautiful, you are. What he is saying is that we don't want someone like that in our lives. We want someone who values herself, yes. She also needs to have room in her life for us. One special woman that allows us to be ourselves, and loves us anyway."

Bolt nodded and smiled. "I've got it bad. I saw a grainy photograph, and I was interested. The next time I see the girl in the photograph, she's lying on a hospital bed and refuses to let me see her eyes. Once you opened those beautiful jewels, I was ready to grab you and find a cave to take you to. All I could think about was making you one of our circle."

He looked toward Scott and Randal while he talked. "We want children; my parents died without the one thing that they'd ever asked me for, a grandchild." He turned back to give her his full attention.

"We can hire a surrogate as we've said before. I won't bring you into this relationship, none of us would, to be a brood mare. My question is, can you love and nurture a child that didn't come from your body?" He walked over to her and crouched down. "I don't even know if you like kids, but I want you to be aware that there will be a few little people involved in this family too. I owe it to my family, and frankly, I've done the research for surrogates. The kid thing and loyalty are my hard lines, other than that; I'm adaptable."

Randal was nodding and laughed a little as he studied Bolt. "We all have a lot to learn about each other. Bolt's right, though; we want a kid or two each, and he's right again when he says that we don't want a brood mare. We can hire a nanny for the children, but if you don't like kids to begin with, we need to go to our corners and lick our wounds. As excited as the picture of you with a swollen belly filled with a child makes me, I would never want you to feel used like that."

Scott had been watching her facial expressions, and he winked at her and grinned. The in-depth emotional discussion where they'd bared their souls to each other was in his thoughts as he announced, "I plan on her being barefoot and pregnant as soon as it can be arranged. I'll buy her a few cookbooks so she can practice cooking while she waits to whelp the kid."

Bolt and Randal both stared at him as if he'd lost his stupid mind. Lucy tried hard not to react, but the laughter couldn't be held back for more than a minute after Scott's declarations.

She tried to hold the loud laughter back by holding a hand over her mouth, but with the way Scott was pretending to look bewildered at her reaction, there was no way to keep the gales of laughter from echoing in the room. It took several minutes for her to calm down enough to shake her head at Scott and smile at Bolt and Randal. They were giving Scott looks like they might be sizing him for a pine box.

"What Scott is saying, not too gracefully I might say, is that we've talked about children. I was raised in a very solitary, almost isolated home. My grandparents raised me as you know, but there were no friends or after school jobs until I turned sixteen, and they kept me on a tight leash even then.

"I hadn't given a thought to the possibility of having a baby; it has been low on my list of things to do in my life. When Alan left me, I wasn't sad for more than a few hours. My ego got smacked a little, but I knew at the time that our breakup was for the best."

She folded her arms around her waistline and shivered. "Yesterday wasn't the first time I've had a breakdown like that. The loss of the baby hit me harder than it should have I guess, but like I told Scott, I never realized how much I wanted a child until the doctor stood next to my bed and told me I'd lost one. I've been alone so long; I just hope I don't smother you all and-"

She stopped talking long enough to smack the table, making them raise their heads from what looked like they might be digesting what she was saying or praying. Either way, she wanted them to listen to her.

"I want kids. I want little arms and legs and spilled cereal, and the whole thing. As long as you agree to help change diapers and walk the floors with a cranky baby, and listen to me when I have something to say, I think we can make this work. I don't know much about babies, but I can learn, and so can you."

The knock on the door put the men's immediate plans to start that family then and there on hold. The man that Lucy had hired to drive the truck of boxes to the apartment was there, and the men were needed to unload the boxes and stack them in the corner of the living room.

Randal hadn't told the other men about buying the house, but Bolt told him that he might as well get the paperwork done for the house. "Look at this place, we need the space, and from what I've seen, we need to arrange to have it painted and updated. So the sooner we have things ready, the sooner we can move in."

Lucy stood in the doorway leading from the kitchen and watched her men stacking the filled boxes behind the treadmill. This was going to work. With love and commitment, they would have a wonderful life together.

Prologue

Bolt was laying across the bed with his head pillowed on his forearm while he watched the faces of Randal and Scott. The sound of the flushing toilet got all of their attention. Lucy held a pregnancy test stick in each hand.

The sound of a crying toddler had her changing direction as she headed towards the door leading to the hallway, and the screaming child. She forgot about the items that she was holding until the men swarmed around her, stopping her before she exited the room.

Randal shook his head. "Lucy, we hired Henry and Fiona to help deal with the kids, and you really need to sit down. You're as pale as a sheet."

When she'd lost her morning coffee, the first thing Scott had done was make a quick run to the drug store for the pregnancy tests. It had become a routine over the years since they'd come together as a family unit. Lucy had given the men five children and never flinched over the fact that she gained thirty or forty pounds each time. She now sported several stretch marks in places that she had never thought to have them, and a few places that her men would not talk about to her.

Bolt gently pulled the white plastic sticks from her fingers, and she shook her head a little to redirect her thoughts.

One of the tests said that she was pregnant; the other was a negative symbol. She knew what that meant. Not just a trip to the gynecologist but probably another set of twins. She decided to throw in the towel.

"If this is another set of twins, I know some men that will be visiting the doctor and taking care of the population explosion around here right?"

The looks of determination on their faces made her smile. Their heads bobbed up and down in agreement, but she wouldn't insist on them getting snipped unless they felt that it was what they wanted to do.

For her part, she loved being pregnant, and while the delivery process was not her favorite thing to do, the tiny, red-faced babies were worth it. They had been together for eight years now, and she had never been happier in her life.

Randal had surprised her when he came home two years ago with a woman that looked slightly familiar to Lucy, but she was shocked when the woman broke down and cried a river of tears when Randal introduced her as her mother.

"I didn't have a job. I was sixteen, and your grandparents were not forgiving. Your father was killed in a car crash, and the man that I was with at the time was abusive. I'm not excusing what I did, and I'm not going to lie to you about my stupidity. I tried to get you back once I got my life stable with a good job and a good man, but my parents refused to let me see you. You have sisters and a brother that you've never met, but I never kept you a secret from them."

The explanation took the entire day, and once Paula had driven away, Lucy tackled Randal and showed her appreciation for his efforts.

Speaking of Randal, Lucy quickly looked at the clock and started pushing through the wall of muscle blocking her path to the door. "Look, Randal's grandparents will be here at two, and we still have to get the house cleaned up, so they don't think you live in a barn."

She was escorted to the bed, and Bolt laid down next to her with his thick arm over her ribcage, so she was pinned to the bed.

"Nap first, Momma; then you can order us around. Randal and I will get the kids to pick up the toys and Bolt needs to take a nap with you to make sure that you rest." Scott leaned down trying to fight the grin on his handsome face. He was always this way when they suspected that she was pregnant. Seeing her belly growing seemed to make him even more attracted to her.

Randal would be following her around and taking anything that weighed more than ten pounds from her arms. He threatened to paddle her like a toddler if he caught her on the step stool changing a lightbulb again.

Bolt made sure that she ate healthily and got plenty of rest. They would all be pains in the ass for nine months, but she would not trade a minute of their affection for anything. Her life was all she'd ever wished for, and she smiled as she snuggled deeper into the strong shoulder cradling her head and neck.

Lynn Ray Lewis

I love writing Erotic Fiction.
Give me peace and quiet or a set of
headphones and a good music library and i will
write until my hands hurt. Then I will lay in bed
and think of what my characters will do or say
next.

By Lynn Ray Lewis

Jody's Men
Regina's Men
Mackie's Men
Lucy's Men

A Place For Her (Hade's Temple Book 1)

I Waited For You (Gaurdians Book 1)

Rane's Giants (Tremble Island Book 1)
Hawk's Nest (Tremble Island Book 2)
Demon's End (Tremble Island Book 3)